Wishes, wishes...

Gryffin looked at me. "What would *you* have asked the Dream-Maker for? That's what I want to know."

I sighed and snuggled deeper into the sofa. My head tilted sideways till it was leaning on Gryffin's shoulder. "So many things," I whispered. "I want my father to do something to prove he cared for me. I want my mother to be happy. I want someone in my family to love me for who I am," I said. "I want you to be well, or at least out of pain. I want Sarah to marry Bo and have a splendid life. I want Mr. Shelby to find every book he's ever wanted to read. I want . . . I want . . . I want everyone I ever met to have at least one wish come true, even if they don't deserve it. That's what I want."

Gryffin was laughing now, silently. I could feel his shoulders shaking. He picked up my hand and held it in front of him, turning it this way and that, as if it was a rare and beautiful stone he had just rescued from a riverbed. "Those are some very generous wishes," he said.

OTHER SPEAK BOOKS

The Company of Swans	Eva Ibbotson
Just Listen	Sarah Dessen
Looking for Alaska	John Green
The Morning Gift	Eva Ibbotson
My Heartbeat	Garret Freymann-Weyr
Prom Anonymous	Blake Nelson
The Safe-Keeper's Secret	Sharon Shinn
SASS: Westminster Abby	Micol Ostow
This Lullaby	Sarah Dessen
The Truth-Teller's Tale	Sharon Shinn

The Dream-Maker's Magic

SHARON SHINN

speak

An Imprint of Penguin Group (USA) Inc.

SPEAK
Published by the Penguin Group
Penguin Group (USA) Inc., 345 Hudson Street, New York, New York 10014, U.S.A.
Penguin Group (Canada), 90 Eglinton Avenue East, Suite 700, Toronto, Ontario, Canada M4P 2Y3
(a division of Pearson Penguin Canada Inc.)
Penguin Books Ltd, 80 Strand, London WC2R 0RL, England
Penguin Ireland, 25 St Stephen's Green, Dublin 2, Ireland (a division of Penguin Books Ltd)
Penguin Group (Australia), 250 Camberwell Road, Camberwell, Victoria 3124, Australia
(a division of Pearson Australia Group Pty Ltd)
Penguin Books India Pvt Ltd, 11 Community Centre,
Panchsheel Park, New Delhi - 110 017, India
Penguin Group (NZ), 67 Apollo Drive, Rosedale, North Shore 0632, New Zealand
(a division of Pearson New Zealand Ltd)
Penguin Books (South Africa) (Pty) Ltd, 24 Sturdee Avenue,
Rosebank, Johannesburg 2196, South Africa

First published in the United States of America by Viking,
a member of Penguin Group (USA) Inc., 2006
Published by Speak, an imprint of Penguin Group (USA) Inc., 2008

1 3 5 7 9 10 8 6 4 2

CIP Data is available.

Speak ISBN 978-0-14-241096-7
Printed in the United States of America

~ FOR ANDREW ~
When you're old enough to read this
May every single one of your dreams come true

Ventures fall to grief;

Hopes collapse in rue.

But fire runs 'round the wreath,

And secret dreams come true.

Part

One

Chapter One

HIS IS THE STORY MY MOTHER TOLD ME: She was traveling late in her pregnancy when she was overcome by labor pains. Fortunately, she was near a small town and had enough time to send a message to my father before she was gripped with spasms so great she could barely speak. A midwife arrived in time to help deliver the baby, a squalling, dark-haired boy. My mother, who had lost a great deal of blood, saw him for only a moment before she slipped into a sleep from which they thought she would not recover. When she woke, my father was there with a wet nurse; they would not let her near the baby till she had regained her own strength. By that time, they were back home, having chanced the two-day journey in the hopes that she would recover better in her own surroundings.

The baby was nearly two weeks old before my mother was strong enough to care for him herself. But the first time she unwrapped his soiled diapers, she began to scream. The baby was not a boy after all, but a girl. My mother could not be calmed from her hysteria. She could not be convinced that, in the birthing bed, she was in no condition to know whether she had delivered herself of a son or a daughter. Nothing my father or the wet nurse said could convince her that she had not borne a boy who had mysteriously metamorphosed into a girl.

I was that baby. I was that strangely altered child.

From that day on, my mother watched me with a famished attention, greedy for clues. I had changed once; might I change again? Into what else might I transform, what other character might I assume? As for myself, I cultivated a demeanor of sturdy stoicism. I was hard to ruffle, hard to incite to anger—at least that anyone could tell from watching me. It was as if I hoped my unvarying mildness would reassure my mother, convince her to trust me. It was as if she was some animal lured from wild lands and I was the seasoned trainer who habitually made no sudden moves.

She never did learn to trust me, though, or to accept me for who I was. It was my first lesson in failure, and it stayed with me the rest of my life.

Every important event of my life seemed to be set in motion during the summer. The year I turned nine, our small town of Thrush Hollow was visited by a Truth-Teller, a thin and haggard woman. Neither her soul nor her body accommodated the padding that sometimes makes life more comfortable. I can't remember who called her to Thrush Hollow or why, though it is always a dangerous gamble to ask Truth-Tellers for their services. They cannot speak lies and they do not indulge in pleasant deceptions. You may find that what they have to say to you is just as unpalatable as what you would have them say to your neighbor.

At any rate, this Truth-Teller had arrived and was staying at the local inn, and a few people had gone to lay their grievances at her feet. One night I overheard an argument between my mother and father, when they thought I was already sleeping, and the next day the three of us headed to the inn. My father, a dark and perpetually harassed man, looked dour and unwilling. My mother, who was short and fair and very determined, seemed nearly as grim. She had wrapped her fingers around my wrist with a grip so tight I kept twisting to get free, but she would not release me. I did not protest aloud, of course. I never said anything that might mark me as temperamental.

When we arrived at the inn, we were directed to a small parlor in the back. It was a warm day, so the windows were open, but the room was still stuffy and hot. The Truth-Teller sat in a straight-backed chair, her eyes closed, her head resting against the worn cushion. She opened her eyes when the three of us walked in, and she did not look happy to see us.

"What is it?" she snapped. "I'm tired. There are enough liars in Thrush Hollow to make even the strongest Truth-Teller weak, and I'm old and frail."

"I won't take much of your time," my mother said breathlessly.

"Introduce yourselves," the old lady demanded.

"I'm Amelia Carmichael. That's my husband, Stephen. That's Kellen." My mother had christened me after an uncle of hers, but it was a name some women bore as well. It was not a name that gave away secrets.

"And what do you want me to tell you, Amelia, except that your agitation is making me nervous?"

"I would just like to ask you a few questions about my son," my mother said, pushing me forward. I was dressed that day, as I was dressed every day, in shapeless clothing that would suit a boy and yet not be wholly out of place on a girl—loose black trousers, loose white shirt, leather shoes. My unstyled black hair hung to my shoulders, its only positive attribute that it was clean. I could have been any anonymous child called in from afternoon play.

The Truth-Teller sat up and stared at me, her dark eyes bright with irritation. I stared back at her, my expression impassive. "Son!" the old woman exclaimed. "This child isn't a boy. It's a girl. Why do you call her 'son'?"

"See, yes, she's a girl *now*, but she wasn't always," my mother said eagerly. "That's what I want you to tell me— that's what I want you to tell my husband. When she was *born*, she was a boy. I saw him. You tell them the truth."

The Truth-Teller gave a crack of laughter. She was still staring at me, and I could read neither compassion nor interest in her eyes. "No, this one was a girl from the moment she was born," the old woman said flatly. "She was a girl inside the womb. She has never been anything else."

My mother fell back with a little cry, her hands going to her cheeks. I saw my father move to stand behind her, as if to lend her support. "But she—but I *saw* him—she has been changed—"

The Truth-Teller closed her eyes again and leaned back against the chair. "Don't waste my time," she said.

My mother babbled a few more incoherent protests, but the Truth-Teller did not look at any of us again. My father turned my mother toward the door and practically hauled her out the inn and down the street to our house. I followed behind them, saying nothing.

I was neither surprised nor unsurprised by the Truth-Teller's words. My life had been so strange up to this point that I would not have found it particularly unnerving to have had my mother's madness proved true. You understand, I had not been treated as a girl at any point in my life—I had not been dressed in frilly gowns or showered with gifts of lace and ribbon. And yet, I had not really been treated as a boy, either, expected to go fishing or frog-hunting with my neighbors. In fact, no one really knew what to make of me. My father tended to avoid me. He was a peddler of metal goods and so he traveled a great deal. When he returned, he was awkward around me, not sure what to say. The people of Thrush Hollow all knew I was a girl, but— since I dressed in such indeterminate clothes, and since my mother *spoke* of me as if I was a boy—sometimes they forgot. So one day I might be greeted as "lad" and another day as "missy," and I found it just as easy to respond to either. I did not really think of myself as a boy or a girl. I considered myself just Kellen. Just me.

Just nobody.

But the Truth-Teller was convinced I was a girl. Had always been a girl. She had not said I always *would* be a girl, and I considered life uncertain enough to reserve as a possibility the idea that someday, even yet, I might assume a shape that better pleased my mother. But for now, one question had been resoundingly answered.

It did not make my life any easier.

That night, as the night before, as many nights in the past, my parents stayed up late, arguing. There was a more urgent quality to the quarrel this night than there usually was; the raised voices were louder, more accusatory. I snuck from my bedroom to crouch in the hallway, listening to them as they paced the parlor and shouted.

"I cannot *do* this any longer, Amelia," my father said, his voice despairing. "I cannot live such a strange and sad life. It is killing me—it is killing all of us."

"Maybe in Wodenderry—there are plenty of Truth-Tellers in the royal city. I will go there with Kellen, and I will ask every one of them—"

"Amelia, you have been told the truth already! Kellen is a girl! She was always a girl! Give up this madness and try to resume some normalcy in your life! When I think what we have put her through—our own daughter—and when I think there is no end to it, I swear to you, I cannot breathe. Make your peace with your destiny and take up the shape of your true life."

"I can't," my mother whispered. "I know I'm right."

There was a long silence. I crept close enough to peek around the corner of the door. I saw my father standing with his head against the wall and his hands flat against the paneling. It looked as if he was holding up the walls of the house, but I knew it was really the other way around.

"Go to sleep," he said finally. "I have to leave again in the morning. We'll talk about this more when I get back."

"And that will be when?"

He shook his head, rubbing his forehead against the paneling. "I don't know. I'll send word."

"I'm not crazy," my mother said.

Still resting against the wall, he turned his head a little to look at her. "You're obsessed," he said. "And you're ruining Kellen's life. And you're ruining your own. And you're ruining mine. Even if you're not crazy, what you're doing is."

"I want Kellen to be what he is supposed to be."

"She will be," my father said. "Whatever that is."

In the morning, he was gone, his cart and his metal goods with him. He usually traveled for seven or ten days at a time and returned exhausted but cheerful, coins jingling in his pocket. He often brought us treats from nearby towns, Tambleham or Merendon or wherever he had gone on his route this time. Once he went all the way to Wodenderry and brought me back a doll shaped like Queen Lirabel. I was always pleased to know he thought of me on the road, since he seemed to think of me so little when we were in the same house.

This time, when he left, he did not return.

Two weeks after his departure, my mother received a note that sent her crying bitterly to her room. It was not unprecedented for my mother to have an emotional breakdown, and

I knew what to do. I fixed dinner for myself, finished up the chores, kept quiet, and allowed her to weep in silence. When I was sure she had sobbed herself to sleep, I crept into her room to wash her face and loosen her dress so that she could pass the night comfortably. It was summer, but the air was cool, so I shut the window and covered her with a sheet.

Then I picked up the note that she had flung to the floor and took it to the parlor to read it by candlelight. It was from my father.

Amelia:

I can't stand our life like this. I have left for the last time, and I'm not coming back. Don't worry about money—I'll send what I can every few weeks. Tell Kellen I love her, even if it has often seemed like I don't. Take care of yourself as best you can.

Stephen

For a moment, I wanted to cry, too, except that I knew it would do no good. Tears would not bring my father back, and tears would not change my mother. Tears would not turn me into someone she could love. I folded the note and went back into her room, carefully dropping the letter on the floor where she had left it. Then I tiptoed to my room, stretched out on my bed, and lay awake till morning.

Chapter Two

nce my father left, there was more for me to do around the house, and I began to take on the chores a son might handle. By the time I was eleven, I was very strong. I could chop wood, haul water, handle awkward and heavy loads, and wring the neck of a chicken if my mother brought a live bird back from market. I also learned the tasks that women taught their daughters—how to cook, how to clean, how to sew. Truthfully, I thought all skills were equally important, and I wondered why they had been, at least among the children of Thrush Hollow, mostly assigned by gender.

I had also come to appreciate the privileges that fell more to boys than to girls, and to take advantage of them when I had the opportunity. For instance, a boy's pair of pants was much less restrictive than a girl's dress, so I continued to wear loose trousers and shirts most of the time. There was no part of town that was off-limits to boys, although girls were discouraged from entering the tavern alone or wandering down certain alleys where gaming was pursued. Boys were expected to earn coins running a variety of errands—fetching a package for the innkeeper, for instance, or holding the reins of a traveler's horse. Girls were never given such opportunities.

As money was scarce in our household, despite the envelopes that came erratically from my father, I was always happy to earn a few extra coppers. Usually I shared them with my mother and they went toward some desperately needed household purchase. Sometimes I kept them for myself and bought an item long coveted. Sweets, usually; toys, sometimes. Once I brought home a gift for my mother, a length of discounted lace from the dressmaker's shop. She cried so hard and thanked me so often that I decided never to make that particular mistake again. Thereafter, I spent all windfalls on myself.

The summer I was eleven, I caught the attention of the new teacher who'd arrived a few weeks early to get the schoolhouse in order. I had helped him carry his bags into the inn, because he was thin and stooped and looked to be asthmatic besides. Not only that, he had to be old enough to be my mother's father. But his round face was pleasant, and he did not look at all stupid.

"Now, what's your name, young fellow?" he asked after he had introduced himself as Ian Shelby and dropped two coins in my hand.

"Kellen Carmichael."

"What grade will you be in this fall?" I looked at him blankly. He elaborated. "How far are you in your schooling?"

"I don't go to school," I said, for I never had. And now,

with my father gone, there was too much to do around the house. It had not seemed to occur to my mother that I might need a formal education, and it had never occurred to me, either.

Ian Shelby looked disapproving. "You have to go to school," he said. "How else will you learn your letters? Your numbers? Your history?"

"I can read," I assured him. My mother had taught me, right along with the sewing and the cooking. "And count. I don't care about history."

"It's always a mistake not to care about history," he said. "How old are you, young—" He hesitated for a moment. "Young woman?" he asked.

I was impressed by his perceptiveness, so I answered. "Eleven. Twelve at the end of summer."

"Eleven-year-old girls should be in school," he said firmly. "If you like, I'll talk to your parents and explain why an education is important."

I laughed. "My mother won't care what you say."

He pulled a pair of spectacles from his pocket and surveyed me with some seriousness. It made me fidgety; I could not tell what his inspection would yield him. "Your mother might be brought to care," was all he said. "I will see you enrolled in school this fall, Kellen Carmichael. See if I don't."

If I had known Ian Shelby better at that moment, I would have resigned myself instantly to the notion that, come autumn, I would be attending the Thrush Hollow Schoolhouse.

His visit to my mother yielded predictable results, for she swore she could not spare her son for the five hours a day school was in session. I was lurking outside the parlor while this conversation took place, and I heard the gap in the conversation that followed while Ian Shelby assimilated this information. But the pause was brief; he smoothly plunged forward.

"What you need from your son today is nothing compared to what he will need from an education tomorrow," the schoolteacher said. "Don't set yourself up as the reason your child might fail in the future."

"He won't fail. He's a smart boy," my mother said. "I need him."

The discussion, which lasted another twenty minutes, ended on the same note. I was standing outside, looking casual and disinterested, when Ian Shelby finally left. He appraised me a moment, and then said, "I was right, wasn't I? You're her daughter, not her son?"

I nodded. "Told you she wouldn't care."

"Oh, don't give up yet," he said. "I haven't. It seems more imperative than ever that you be allowed formal schooling."

I wasn't sure what "imperative" meant, though I came to think it meant inevitable. Ian Shelby talked to the town mayor, he talked to the parents of other children my age, and the result was that enough pressure was brought to bear on my mother that she had no choice but to allow me to attend school that fall.

You understand, I was not sure this was a victory.

I hated school for the first few weeks. I was not used to being confined in any one place, and I missed the freedom of doing whatever I wanted once the household chores were done. Sitting still was hard; *learning* was even harder, for Ian Shelby had high standards and was not inclined to accommodate laziness in his students. At times I could actually feel my head expand from all the new knowledge he was attempting to cram inside of it.

Then there were my fellow students.

I knew all of them by sight, of course, but I wouldn't have counted any one of them as a friend. Well, I was a strange girl; I was not easy to take to. This had been true in random encounters on the streets of Thrush Hollow, and it was still true inside the schoolhouse.

We had been divided loosely by grade and ability into three levels. I sat with the lowest group, with children my age and much younger, practicing my letters and learning more complicated words than had come my way so far. The children in this particular cluster were mostly too young to have developed the art of teasing with any real skill. The oldest students were busy flirting with or ostracizing one another, and they paid no attention to anyone outside their own small circle. But those in the middle group had enough attention and enough malice for everybody.

"Hey. Who's the new boy?" was the question that came up as soon as we were sent outside for our mid-morning break on the very first day.

"Kellen Carmichael," someone answered.

13

"You. Kellen. Can you run?"

"Run well enough," I said in a wary voice.

"Going to do relay races. You want to play?"

I shrugged. "All right."

"I don't want girls on our team," said a weasely dark-haired boy.

Everyone stared. "That's a girl?" several boys asked.

"Yes," I said defiantly. "I can still run."

"We've had girls on our team before," said a tall boy.

"I don't want girls! You can have them on your team."

"Are you *sure* she's a girl? Looks like a boy."

"I can run faster than you can," I said to the weasely boy. I had no idea if this was true. But I was fast enough to be respectable and willing to prove it.

"I don't race girls," he said.

I shrugged. "I'll race someone else, then."

That was good enough for the others, and they picked their champion, a burly fair-haired boy with a stupid grin. The weasely one called out our marks and shouted "Go!" and we were off. I was smaller and had better wind; he had more powerful legs, but the course was short. I won. A few of the onlookers cheered and a few booed.

"She can run on my team," the tall boy said. "Let's pick sides."

I handled my part of the relay with speed and competence, and the first recess went well enough. So did the second one. So did the playground breaks for the entire first week. But there were still questions about me. The weasely boy, whose name was Carlon, never stopped needling me and was always ready with a laugh or a sneer if I fell. He and his friends would whisper together, and throw me dark looks, and altogether give me the sense that they were plotting against me. Of course, they did the same to everyone who was smaller and weaker than they were. They were born bullies and no doubt had long careers of cruelty ahead of them.

I would have abandoned the boys' games except that the girls' circles were closed to me. A few times that first week I attempted to play or eat lunch with the girls my age, and each time I was rebuffed. The prettiest of them actually squealed and leapt to her feet when I sat on the ground next to her one afternoon.

"Oooh—she's so strange—don't let her touch me!" she cried. Some of her friends giggled, and some of them cast me considering looks, and none of them talked to me. "Make her go away!"

"Go play with the boys, *Kellen*," one of her friends said, emphasizing my name as if it was an ugly word. "We don't want you here."

I stood up, turned away, turned back, and shoved the pretty girl onto the ground. She squealed again, a most satisfying sound, as her pale pink frock went skidding into the mud.

Naturally, Ian Shelby was informed of the infraction. After class, he gave me a grave lecture on civility.

"I'll be nice to them when they're nice to me," was my response. "Which will be never. So I guess I'll just have to quit school."

"Not yet," he said.

The next week was better, for I was good at the games the boys played. I could throw a ball and hit with a stick as well as any of them, and I had already proved I was a runner. But I was woefully inept at boxing, a sport introduced the third week of school, and I ended up down in the mud myself, gasping for breath and feeling bruises form on every edge of my body.

"*Told* you she was a girl," Carlon said, because there had been renewed debate on this topic when I had won a footrace that very morning.

"Prove it," one of his cronies suggested.

I tried to scramble to my feet, but too late. Too many hands. Arms holding my shoulders down, fingers in my waistband, my pants pulled down to my knees. No doubt about it now.

"I *hate* girls," one of Carlon's friends grumbled as everybody released me and turned away, no longer interested. "Hey, where's the ball? Let's see how far we can kick it."

I sat up, pulled my pants back on, and willed myself not to cry. A boy wouldn't have cried. Most girls wouldn't have been racing to begin with. How was I supposed to behave? Where was I supposed to find my friends? I waited for Mr. Shelby to ring the bell signaling end of recess, and I fiercely regretted any necessity for acquiring an education.

Chapter Three

he next day, right before he sent everyone else outside for the morning break, Mr. Shelby said, "Oh, and I want two students to assist me. I received a shipment of books from an old friend, and I need help organizing them. Whoever volunteers will have to stay in during recess for the next few days, if that's all right. Kellen, will you be one of them?"

I looked up in surprise. What a fortunate reprieve! I had been uneasy about what this day's playground activity might consist of. "I suppose," I said.

Mr. Shelby nodded. "Good. And Gryffin? Can I count on you?"

Every head swiveled to stare at the student sitting in the back. He never joined any of our games at recess, anyway. He was a lame boy who walked very slowly, using two canes. No one would ever think to challenge *him* to a footrace. He was about my age, but in the level above me. I had never said a word to him in my life.

"Yes, of course," he replied.

"Good. Everyone else—out you go."

The room emptied of everyone except the teacher, the boy, and me. Mr. Shelby lowered his thin, stooped frame till he was kneeling by a battered trunk in the back of the room, muttering when he could not get the lock to spring. "I must have left the key in my jacket pocket," he said, rising and heading for the door. "I'll be back in a few moments."

He disappeared, and the boy and I were left alone. Curious, I hitched my desk closer to Gryffin's and studied him a minute. He had nondescript brown hair, badly cut, and a thin face. Everything about him was thin, even his arms and fingers, though his shoulders looked bulky under his plain cotton shirt. I guessed his arms were strong from wielding the canes and supporting the weight that his legs could not. His eyes were a startling blue, and his face was alive with interest.

"Gryffin?" I said tentatively. "That's your name?"

He nodded. "You're Kellen. I've seen you around town."

I was surprised. "Really? I haven't seen you."

He smiled a little ruefully. "Mostly I watch from the window."

"What window?"

"My uncle Frederick runs the tavern in the square. I have a room on the second floor."

"Must be hard to get upstairs," I said without thinking.

But he only nodded. "Once I go up, I don't usually come down for much. So I look out the window instead."

"Why do you live with your uncle?"

"Because everyone else is dead." He considered for a

moment. "Well, my father might not be dead. But he's gone."

Now I was the one to nod. "Yeah. So's my father."

"Yeah," he said. "I heard."

"And my mom's crazy," I offered.

He smiled again, more widely. "I heard that, too."

"So maybe having an uncle is better than having a parent."

His face took a shuttered look. "It doesn't seem like it."

I gestured toward the floor. "So what happened to your foot?"

"Feet. And legs," he corrected. He shrugged a little. "Twisted somehow, when I was born. They've never been right."

"Are they getting better?"

"Getting worse, it seems like."

"Do they hurt?"

He nodded. "Most of the time."

"Have you seen a doctor?"

"In Thrush Hollow? I'd have to go to Wodenderry to find someone who could help. And my uncle doesn't have the money to pay for doctors. Anyway"—he shrugged again—"I don't think anyone can mend me."

"Did a Truth-Teller tell you that?" I demanded. "Because unless a Truth-Teller said it, you might be wrong. Someone could help you."

He looked amused. "Thrush Hollow doesn't even have its own Safe-Keeper," he said. "It's too small to draw Truth-Tellers."

"What you really need is the Dream-Maker," I said, inspired. "When you go to Wodenderry, don't look for a doctor. Look for the Dream-Maker. Tell her you want your legs to be strong. She'll make your wish come true."

"I don't think I'll be going to Wodenderry any time soon."

"Maybe she'll come here. You can make your wish then. She travels all the time."

"To Thrush Hollow?" he said with the same disbelieving inflection.

"Well, *some* Dream-Maker must have come here *some*time. I thought Dream-Makers went everywhere in the kingdom?"

"Melinda's getting pretty old by now," Gryffin said. "I don't think she travels much."

"Well, I don't think you should give up," I said.

"I think I'll count on something other than magic to fix my life," he said.

"Like what? Fix it how?"

"I'm pretty smart," he said, the way another boy might have said *I'm pretty tall* or *My hair is red*. "When I'm old enough, I want to apply to the university in Wodenderry. I'll study law or accounting, and then I'll get a job in the royal city. Maybe I'll do clerking for the king." He gave a smile; that had been a joke. But he sobered immediately and glanced around the schoolroom. "That's why I'm here. I have to learn as much as I can."

"I'm here because Mr. Shelby made me come," I said darkly.

"It wouldn't hurt you to learn something, too," he said.

I rolled my eyes. "And then what? What kind of job am I going to be good for? No one's going to want to hire me."

"You can do whatever you want," Gryffin said, with such certainty that I almost stared. How could someone with mighty few advantages be so sure that he could determine his own future? How could he think that *I* had any chance to do so? Had I been in his place, I would have been sulky and bitter. As it was, I was hardly optimistic and sunny. "You just have to know what it is you want."

"Something better than this," I said. That wasn't particularly specific, but Gryffin nodded. Better than Thrush Hollow. Better than lost or neglectful parents, better than pain of the body and pain of the soul.

"But it starts here," he said. "That's why we have to learn everything we can."

"I'm not a boy, you know," I said abruptly. "I'm a girl."

"I know," he said.

"You haven't asked why I don't act like a girl."

He turned his head to give me an appraising look out of those blue eyes. "What does a girl act like?" he said.

"What I mean is—"

"I know what you mean."

At that particular moment, Mr. Shelby bustled back in, triumphantly jingling a key ring from one bony hand. "Here it is!" he said. "Not that you'll have time to do any work today, since it's almost time for me to ring the bell. You'll just have to stay in a few more afternoons and help me sort through the books."

He never said, and we never asked, but I assumed Mr. Shelby had kept us inside that day to protect us from the harassment of our fellow students. I had not paid any attention to Gryffin's forays outside the building, but I guessed they had been even less pleasant than my own. It was a kindness on Mr. Shelby's part to keep us indoors, a way of sheltering us from spitefulness without having to chastise our abusers. I had missed the chance to run and jump and expend some of my considerable energy—but talking to Gryffin had been a more than acceptable exchange.

I knew already that he would be my friend. My first. Perhaps even then I suspected that his friendship would become the standard by which every other one was measured.

Within a matter of days, Gryffin and I were inseparable. I would swing by his uncle's tavern in the morning on my way to the schoolhouse and walk slowly alongside Gryffin until we made it to the building, talking about anything that caught our attention. Most days he was animated and cheerful, interested in everything, from trash we saw on the side of the road to my observations about the people we passed. Occasionally, when he was in more pain than usual, he could be sharp-tongued and grim, and I learned to be silent those days so as not to earn a biting retort to an innocuous observation. I have to say, however, on balance I was in a bad mood more often than Gryffin was, and he tolerated my outbursts with general good humor. So I tried to do the same for him.

The first few days we walked to school together, I carried his books and his lunch for him. Then it occurred to me there was an easier way, and I spent an evening designing and sewing a knapsack that he could wear over his shoulders. Stupid that his uncle had never thought to make him such a thing before, and Gryffin was delighted with it. Now he started borrowing books from Mr. Shelby, bringing home novels and historical accounts and advanced mathematics texts, and studying into the night. When he came across something he found particularly interesting, he would share it with me the next day. Thus, somewhat against my will, I learned the chronology of our major kings and queens, the history of our foreign trade, a handful of poems, and the basics of long division.

Because there were now two of us, the other students mostly left us alone. Gryffin was not above tripping somebody with one of his canes if he thought he had been insulted or I had been maligned, and I was willing to swing wildly in an attempt to strike someone if I had been hit first. There were still the occasional taunts and ambushes, but they were rare and minor—and everybody had to endure those once in a while.

Unfortunately for me, Gryffin was such an excellent student that occasionally Mr. Shelby called on him for help tutoring the younger children. Those sessions usually took place during lunch or recess, leaving me alone during breaks in the school day. Most of the time I got along all right, sometimes joining the running games. Once in a while some of the middle-grade boys would corner me and pick a fight, despite the fact that I made sure I was never the only one injured in such encounters.

In fact, I had just slammed Carlon's best friend to the ground one afternoon when a firm voice interrupted our quarrel. "Stop it! Both of you! Carlon, I'm going to tell your father how you've been behaving."

"She's the one who started it," Carlon said, panting a little as he shoved me in the arm. I slapped at his hand, but without much force. I was eyeing the young woman who had interrupted us.

Her name was Sarah Parmer, and she was probably seventeen. She was as tall as any of the boys and generously built, and for a moment I was hopeful that she would punch Carlon on my behalf, because she could surely do some damage. But it really just took one good look at her gentle face and serene demeanor to conclude that Sarah Parmer was not the kind of girl who engaged in brawls on the school grounds—or anywhere else, for that matter.

"Don't bother lying," she said to Carlon. "You started it. She was defending herself. Why don't you just leave her alone?"

Carlon hunched a shoulder. His friend had by this time climbed to his feet and was investigating a long tear in his sleeve. "I don't like her. Acts strange and dresses funny," he said.

"At least I'm not stupid and ugly like you are," I shot back.

Sarah gave me a reproving look from dark eyes. "Kellen, you just make it worse."

"Some days it couldn't *be* worse," I retorted.

"You boys go off now," she said. "I want to talk to Kellen."

Carlon sneered, but sauntered away, followed by his companion. I looked with some wariness up at Sarah Parmer. "What do you want to talk to me about?"

She looked suddenly shy and uncertain. "I thought you might do me a favor."

This was unique in my experience. "Me? What kind of favor?"

"I'm not learning my numbers, and I need to know them. Can your friend Gryffin help me, do you think?"

I stared. "He only teaches the little kids."

"Well, do you think he could teach me, too?"

I examined my forearm, which was bleeding. "I guess he could. I'll ask him." I looked at Sarah Parmer again. "Do you want to stay in at recess?"

"No," she said quickly, and I was sure she didn't want any of the girls in her own grade to know that she was seeking assistance from a younger student. "Maybe he could come to my house after school a couple days a week."

I knew that her parents ran a little freighting company located at the edge of town. "It's pretty far for him to walk," I said.

"My father could send a cart."

I thought Gryffin would like that. "And take him home again?"

"Of course."

"I'll ask him," I said.

"I would pay him something, of course."

"*Really?*" It hadn't occurred to me this could be a money-making proposition. "I wonder if I know anything you need to learn."

Sarah Parmer actually laughed. She was not an especially pretty girl; her dark brown hair was wrapped in a braid around her head, and her face was broad and plain. But she had an appealing laugh, and I smiled in response. "What do you know how to do?"

"I can cook. I can sew. I can work in the garden. I can fix a broken chair if it only needs a few nails in it."

"Know anything about horses?"

I was disappointed. "No."

"Well, there's always other work to do. Why don't you come out with Gryffin tomorrow and we'll see if my mother or father can find some odd jobs for you?"

"Sure, I can do that," I said, as if I were doing her a kindness.

She nodded, as if she thought so, too. "Thanks. Tomorrow after school, then?"

"I guess so."

Gryffin wasn't quite as dazzled at the invitation as I was, though he was curious to see what life was like at the Parmer house and happy to do what he could to explain the mysteries of math to Sarah. We didn't really have gentry in Thrush Hollow, where pretty much everyone was working poor, but there were a few families who possessed a little more money and ran somewhat more successful enterprises than the rest. The Parmers were among them. The freighting company did steady business through all seasons; Josh Parmer employed two drivers as well as his three sons. Their house, situated in the northern part of town, had always appeared large and comfortable from the outside. We were pleased to have a chance to see inside.

My mother was also delighted at the thought that I might be developing a relationship with the Parmers. "You could be a driver for them someday," she suggested. "Tell Josh Parmer you're good with horses."

"I've never even ridden one."

"Show him what a strong young man you are," she said. "Act responsibly. If you impress him, he'll remember you when he's hiring, no matter what the job is."

It sounded like reasonable advice to me.

The following day, Gryffin and I enjoyed our short ride from the schoolhouse to the Parmer home in the back of a well-sprung wagon. The driver, a cheerful fellow with a bristling red beard, came around to the back of the cart once we'd stopped. We were in front of the whitewashed, two-story house where the Parmers lived. There was a sprawl of barns and other outbuildings behind the house, and several pastures filled with horses grazing.

"You need a hand out of there, buddy?" the driver asked in a genial voice, and before Gryffin could answer a polite "no," the man had lifted the boy from the bench to the street. I could tell that Gryffin was a little ruffled and trying hard not to be angry.

"You didn't need to do that," he said in a quiet voice. "I can manage on my own."

"Oh, well, thought this was easier," the driver said so cheerfully that it was hard to dislike him. "What about those canes? You need those, too?"

Sarah, who had ridden in front with the driver, led us into the house. "All my brothers are on the road, so it ought to be quiet for a change," she told us over her shoulder. "When they're here—well, let's just say it gets a little noisy."

I stared around me as we entered the front door, taking in as many details as I could. All the rooms were bigger and grander than the rooms in my mother's house. Nonetheless, the furniture looked a little worn and much-used, and the colors of the curtains and the sofas were warm and welcoming. It was the sort of house a person would love to come home to, I thought. Nothing at all like my own.

"Sarah, is that you and your friends?" a voice called, and then Betsy Parmer came from the back of the house and joined us in the parlor. She looked just like Sarah—big and broad and gentle—except twenty years older and a little heavier. "Is anybody hungry?"

"Yes," Gryffin and I said together.

Sarah introduced us, and Betsy Parmer shook our hands as if we were important townsfolk, not schoolchildren. "Kellen Carmichael?" she repeated, looking me over a little uncertainly. "You're one of the boys Sarah knows from school?"

"That's right," I said, but Sarah corrected her.

"One of the girls."

28

Betsy Parmer raised her eyebrows at me.

"One of the girls," I admitted.

"And you've come to help Sarah with her numbers?"

"No, I'm not very good at math," I said breezily. "But I thought—if you had chores to do around the house—I'm pretty good at things. I could work while Gryffin gives lessons to Sarah."

I saw Betsy exchange looks with her daughter. "Always plenty to do around here," she said with a laugh. "Why don't you come back to the kitchen with me and we'll see what kind of work we can find."

Chapter Four

he next two months were among the best of my life so far. Autumn was slowly spinning into winter, so the air was crisp and delicious, and the world was drenched in color. My mother, who disliked winter, always grew quieter during this time of year, less unreasonable; it was as if she saved all her strength just for surviving the dark, still season. I had finally settled into school, not just learning key subjects but forming true friendships and learning to avoid the malcontents.

And there was the Parmer house to go to two or three times a week. Betsy always had food ready for us—yellow cheese, fresh bread, fruit pie, or the occasional more substantial dish. While Sarah and Gryffin studied in the parlor, I worked around the kitchen with the matriarch of the house. She was rather impressed with my range of skills and would put me to work at any task I was willing to undertake. I sewed curtains, darned socks, chopped firewood, weeded the garden, scrubbed the oven, fed the chickens, plucked them if they'd been slaughtered for an evening meal, and did any other chore that presented itself.

When Sarah's brothers were home, they filled the house with big bodies and loud laughs and constant conversation, and I found them a little intimidating at first. But, as you might imagine, neither Betsy nor Sarah was the type to tolerate teasing or abuse, so there was nothing to fear from them. They treated me like a younger brother and would ruffle my hair or call me by various nicknames. They treated Gryffin like a rather exotic pet, gingerly but with a certain respect. Josh Parmer was rarely around, for the business took most of his attention, but the few times I saw him I thought him one of the most likable men I'd ever met, genial and honest. In fact, what I really thought was that he deserved to have such a good-hearted wife, such agreeable offspring, such a happy life.

I had to wonder what kind of person I would have been now if I had been born into this house and raised among these people. Would I have been full of laughter myself? Would I have been friendlier with the world, less suspicious, filled with an unconscious optimism? Would I be generous, more willing to hazard myself, secure in the knowledge that love awaited me no matter how dark my day?

Or would I still have been just me?

Gryffin and I had been working at the Parmer house for about a month when I became convinced I was going to die. I had woken up with a small amount of blood on my sheets, which puzzled me because I couldn't remember a wound or find a cut, but I cleaned myself up and went to school. Twice that day I found more blood in my underwear, and as the day progressed, I felt a thick, dull pain build up in the region of my stomach. What could this be? I was panicked and afraid, seized by the notion that I had contracted some disease of the internal organs that would be impossible to cure. Sitting in the classroom, unable to concentrate on Mr. Shelby's lecture, I was overtaken by a great feeling of sadness as I pictured my mother's lonely life—husband missing, only child dead so young. My stomach knotted with pain, and I thought some of it might be coming from the tears I was trying to hold back.

"You're quiet today," Gryffin commented later as we rode in the cart to the Parmer house.

"Just—tired, I suppose," I said in a subdued voice. What a loss to Gryffin, too, if his best friend should die so unexpectedly! I couldn't bear to tell him.

"Well, maybe we'll go home early," he replied.

As usual, once we were at the house, we separated, Gryffin following Sarah to the parlor while I went to the kitchen to see what Betsy needed. Fortunately it was a day of tasks that were not too strenuous—sewing, mostly—and I sat quietly with my hands busy and my thoughts dark.

When I got up once to use the chamber pot, it seemed I filled it instantly with blood.

I pulled my trousers up and stood there, shivering, my arms folded tightly across my chest. How quickly would the disease progress? How many days did I have left? How—how—*how*—could I tell my mother what had happened to me? Or had the same disease infected her already? Maybe it was a plague that would take the whole town. Maybe we were all just a week or two away from a painful and lingering death.

"Kellen! What's wrong?" Betsy had come to look for me and now stood in the doorway of the back room, her face a study in concern. "You look so pale. Do you have a fever?"

"Betsy," I whispered. "I think I'm dying."

She made an inarticulate noise and hurried over to check my forehead with a cool hand. "You don't feel hot. Does your stomach hurt? What's wrong?"

I could hardly get the words out. "I'm bleeding. From the inside."

I gestured toward the chamber pot and then put a hand on my stomach. Her eyes followed the motion of my hand and then fixed on my face. I will never forget the range of expressions she showed then—surprise, comprehension, compassion, and anger. "Kellen," she said very quietly, "has your mother never told you about the monthly bleeding that women experience?"

My mother had never told me about *anything* that women experienced. I shook my head, feeling a slight tendril of hope. Betsy didn't appear as alarmed as I thought she would have if she believed my situation was grave.

"Oh, you poor child," Betsy said, drawing me into a quick hug. "Let me give you some blood rags and some clean clothes—and explain some things to you. Nothing is wrong with you. Everything is just fine. You're just—you're just a young girl, that's all, and this is one of the things that happens to young girls. It's a good thing, really it is. Oh, I'm so glad you were here and I could take care of you."

I was glad of that, too, so relieved to not be facing the prospect of death that I could forgive my mother for not warning me about this most curious fact of life. Betsy didn't forgive her, though; I could tell. Betsy never said a word against my mother—or, indeed, against anyone else—in my hearing. But I could tell she thought my mother unnatural, even cruel. It gave me some comfort to know that, if there was an odd creature living in my house, Betsy did not think I was the strange one. Betsy thought I was an ordinary girl.

Up until Wintermoon, there were only three times Gryffin and I missed our twice-weekly visit to the Parmer homestead. Once was when the whole Parmer house was down with influenza and Sarah warned us not to come over. Once was when my mother caught the very same infection, and I had to stay home to nurse her.

Once was when Gryffin was in too much pain to go.

I hadn't thought much about it that morning when I stopped at his uncle's tavern on my way to school. Usually Gryffin was waiting for me outside, or just inside the door on cold days. This morning he was nowhere in sight, and it was a good ten minutes before someone answered my pounding at the back door. Taverns tended to be open late at night, so those who staffed it were not traditionally early risers. I knew it, but I kept knocking anyway. Eventually the door was opened by Gryffin's aunt, a thin, hollow-eyed woman with stringy hair. She was wearing a nightdress and looked ill-tempered.

"What do you want?" she snapped.

"Gryffin. I walk to school with him."

Her face softened a bit; she actually looked sad. "Oh. I'm afraid he won't be going to school today."

"Why not? Is he sick?"

She hesitated a moment before answering. "His legs are bothering him, that's what," she said. "He can't walk that far."

I hitched my book bag on my shoulder. "Well—should I come by tonight? And see how he's doing? I can bring his assignments so he won't fall behind."

"I don't know if he'll be much better tonight," she said doubtfully.

"I'll come by anyway," I said. "Just to see."

"If you want to," she said, and shut the door in my face.

At school, I told Sarah that Gryffin was unavailable for the evening tutoring session but that I hoped he'd be well in a couple of days. At lunch and during the play periods, I lurked in the shadows of the schoolhouse, hoping to escape attention. Two of the little girls whom Gryffin tutored came and sat with me, and that was all right. Carlon and his friends didn't usually bother me if I had any audience at all. But the girls insisted on playing some elaborate imaginary game that involved them meeting a prince at some Summermoon ball. This required them to describe in great detail the fabulous dresses they would wear at the event, and I was really quite bored. At the afternoon break, I spent the entire period teaching them how to throw a rock with enough accuracy that they could actually hit something ten yards away, and I, at least, enjoyed that much more.

After school, I gathered up my books, accepted Gryffin's assignment from Mr. Shelby, and headed back to the tavern. No one answered my knock this time, either, but I knew the household was up. It was early afternoon, but people were already coming into the tavern for an afternoon drink or an early dinner. No doubt Gryffin's aunt and uncle were too busy to even hear me.

I pushed experimentally at the door and found it unlocked, so I opened it and stepped inside. I was instantly in a dark hallway that led in several directions—down to a cellar, up to the second story, and out to what had to be the kitchens. The smells were strong and appealing, of onions sizzling and meat baking and beer brewing. I could hear a range of voices, near enough to be in the kitchen, far enough to be coming from the taproom. Everyone sounded quite jolly.

I slipped around the newel post and crept upstairs. Here another hallway, longer than the first, offered three doors for me to choose from. Surely one of them opened into Gryffin's room, but which one? I knew that he liked to watch the town square from an upper-story window, so I paused to try to correlate the interior geography of the house with the layout of the streets below. The second room on the right seemed the most likely candidate, so I tiptoed down the hall and quietly knocked.

The silence from within seemed startled for a moment, then Gryffin's voice said, "You can come in." I pushed the door open and went inside.

The room was fairly dark, for it was on the other side of the house from where the sun was sinking toward the horizon. I could see Gryffin, though, hunched on an old ottoman as he sat by the window. His knees were drawn up almost to his chin, and his arms were wrapped protectively around his ankles. His face, which showed surprise at my appearance, also showed a bruise and a nasty cut.

"Kellen," he said. "I wasn't expecting to see you."

I came closer to inspect him. "What happened to *you*?" I said. "Did you fall down the steps?"

He hesitated, and I realized he was considering a lie. Which made me feel peculiar. By this time, Gryffin and I had known each other only about two months, so we still were comparative strangers. But I would have staked any amount of money I could have scraped up that he had never told me a falsehood. I was so used to living a lie that I tended to be sensitive to the truth.

But then he shook his head, and I knew he was going to be honest. "No," he said. "My uncle Frederick hit me."

My eyes widened, and I bent down to get a better look. "*Hit* you," I repeated. "He did more than *hit* you. He really thrashed you."

Wearily, Gryffin nodded.

"What did he do?" I demanded. "When I came to the door this morning, your aunt—I don't know her name—"

"Dora."

"She said your legs were hurting. That's why you couldn't go to school."

He nodded, a flash of bitterness in his eyes. "Well, she was right. They were hurting."

"Did he hit you on your *legs*?" I exclaimed. "What did he *do*?"

"My legs, my face, my shoulders," Gryffin said. "Usually he knocks me down, and he kicks me in the knee and—"

"*Usually*? He's done this before?"

Gryffin just looked at me. His normally sunny face was as closed and uninformative as mine could ever be.

"I hate him," I whispered.

Gryffin shrugged. "I hate him, too," he said, his voice quiet but fierce. "And he hates me. Crippled boy he had to take in because there was no one else. I can't even do any work to help pay my way. The only reason he doesn't throw me out of the house is that the whole town knows I'm here. Folks would talk. Right now they admire him for doing right by his brother's boy. I hear people say it all the time."

"People should know that he beats you up!" I said hotly.

"Well, half of them probably beat their own sons and wives and daughters," he said, still brooding. "They wouldn't be so shocked."

"How badly are you hurt?" I asked. "Will you be able to come to school tomorrow?"

"Probably. People will see the bruise on my face, though."

"Let them see it. Tell them how you got it."

Gryffin's face showed a scowl. "It's too humiliating."

"You told *me* the truth."

He nodded. "I wanted you to know. It's better when someone knows. Just not everyone."

"Someday he'll be sorry," I said ominously.

Gryffin shook his head. "Someday I'll be out of here. At the university in Wodenderry. Or *somewhere*. It won't matter then."

"And I'll be lady-in-waiting to the queen," I said rudely. That made him smile, just a little. I dropped my bag to the floor, knelt beside it, and pulled out some books. "Mr. Shelby gave me these to give to you. This is the story we read in class. And we did some math problems, but he said you wouldn't have any trouble with them, so you shouldn't worry about them. And there was some history, but it was boring. So all you really need is to read this story."

"Thank you, Kellen," he said gravely, but the smile lingered in his eyes. "I feel as if I didn't miss a minute of class."

The next day Gryffin returned to school. He earned a few sideways glances from the younger students, and a rather searching interrogation from Sarah, but he told everyone the story he had almost told me. One of his canes had slipped on the stairs and he had tumbled painfully down. He was better now, yes, though his ankle was twisted and it was even harder to walk than it usually was. Mr. Shelby allowed him to stay in at recess, and allowed me to sit beside him, even though there was no one to tutor and no chores to do for the teacher. Merely, it was a kindness. Within three days, the most visible cuts and bruises were healed, though I noticed that Gryffin still walked with an extra stiffness.

From then on, it seemed, Gryffin was a little less mobile in general, as if he had sustained some permanent damage from those careless blows. I wondered if he had perhaps broken a bone without realizing it, as the fresh pain was masked by the ongoing familiar ache, and if that bone had knitted itself back together in an imperfect fashion. The incident reminded me of how fragile Gryffin could be— something, oddly enough, I had forgotten as soon as we became friends. His mind was so lively, his conversation so informed, that he had a palpable presence; his personality always struck me with an almost physical force. It was true he couldn't walk or run or play like other boys, but I never thought about that when I was with him. With Gryffin, it was so easy to overlook what he couldn't do—or, at least, it was easy for *me*. I suppose other people saw him as broken and a little sad. I saw him as astonishing.

Chapter Five

It snowed for the entire week before Wintermoon. With the ground so icy and treacherous, it was impossible for Gryffin to walk even the short distance between the tavern and the schoolhouse, so he missed every class that week. I accepted books and assignments from Mr. Shelby and carried them to Gryffin's house every night, parroting back to him what I remembered from class. Then we would sit at the window and watch the snow come down like so many tumbled feathers. It was magical to watch the sunlight fade and the darkness flow over the town, thwarted only at random intervals by bright points of candlelight in the windows of the surrounding houses. The snow lay over everything like a veil, hiding cold mysteries.

"Sarah says the snow's so deep on the north road that her father can't get the wagons out," I told Gryffin. "It's better going south, but not by much."

"So everyone will have to stay in town for Wintermoon," he said.

I rubbed at the fogged windowpane. I could hear my

unconvincingly careless tone come to my voice. "Does your uncle do much to celebrate Wintermoon?" I asked.

"Well, the tavern's pretty full Wintermoon Eve," Gryffin said. "A lot of folks come in to drink to midwinter. So my uncle doesn't have time to build a bonfire or anything. What about you and your mother?"

"We used to have a bonfire, when my father was here. But these days . . ." I shrugged. "It's too much of a bother. Make a fire, stay up all night tending it—it was fun when there was someone to share it with, but my mother's always in bed early."

"Do you make a wreath?" he said.

I laughed. "I hadn't thought about that. I suppose you could make a wreath even if you didn't have a bonfire. What would you tie onto yours?"

He thought that over. "Something that meant freedom. A bird feather, maybe. Something to represent happiness. Something for travel. What about you?"

"Money. Happiness. Love," I recited. Who wouldn't want those things?

"Well, I don't see why we can't make our own wreath," Gryffin said. "It could be a really small one. You'd have to gather all the pieces, of course, but we could burn it in the grate in my room."

I was sitting on the floor next to Gryffin's ottoman, but now I practically bounced where I sat. "What a wonderful idea! I'll go through my mother's ragbag and see what I can find. And I'll cut some branches from the spruce tree in the square. Maybe some holly—there's some down the street.

There are plenty of things I can find for us to braid into a wreath."

"Will you be able to come over on Wintermoon? And stay till midnight?" The wreaths were always burned as the hour struck twelve. A way to welcome in the new year the very minute it stumbled into the world.

I shrugged. "Sure. Why not?"

"Maybe your mother will worry?"

"She won't know I'm gone."

He smiled. "This might be my best Wintermoon ever."

The next two days were not school days. I spent my mornings working around the house, helping my mother with the holiday baking, and then I prowled through Thrush Hollow, looking for symbols. Traditionally, Wintermoon wreaths were woven from spruce, cedar, and rowan, but I didn't want to go far afield to the wooded areas a few miles outside of town. Instead, I contented myself with what the local trees had thrown down during recent storms. Half-buried in snow, I found switches of willow and sprays of holly, inflexible oak limbs and springier maple branches. I even cut some live branches down from a kirrenberry tree still growing before the house where a Safe-Keeper used to live. Everybody knew that kirrenberries signified silence, and Safe-Keepers were famous for never breaking theirs.

Some people said that when you burned something on a Wintermoon wreath, you were asking for a particular wish to be granted. Others said, no, sending something up in flames meant you wanted to free yourself from the influence of that specific item. If I brought in a length of kirrenberry, would I be begging to keep my secrets or hoping to leave them behind?

I didn't pause long to wonder; there was too much else to do. As I headed home, I saw the skeleton of a rosebush poke its bones above the drift line of snow, so I trimmed off a few thorny inches and stuffed them into my bag. Here and there, bird feathers lay like discarded jewels along a white coverlet, so I claimed these as well. Someone had lost a shoe buckle in the street. I didn't know what it might stand for, but I liked its silver twinkle, so that went into my bag with the rest.

My mother was making dinner when I returned home. "Goodness, what do you have there? The neighbors' kindling pile?" she asked me.

"No—just a few things I picked up outside," I said.

Incurious as always, she merely said, "Well, get the table set. Dinner's almost ready."

She had made a special meal for Wintermoon and seemed happy as she served it. These past few months she had been doing piecework for a local seamstress, and while she liked the money, the close, painstaking work was hard on her hands and eyes. Like everyone else in the whole world, she had been granted a holiday on Wintermoon and the reprieve made her cheerful. We ate meat pie and fresh bread and lemon cake, and toasted each other with apple cider.

"Any Wintermoon wish?" she asked me.

"A new pair of gloves," I said. I had accidentally found

them in her closet one day, so I knew that was the gift I would find before the parlor fire in the morning.

She laughed. "I meant in the larger sense," she said gaily. "You know. You want to go to sea as a sailor, you want to marry a nice girl and have a family . . . ?"

I smiled. "I want to pass into the next grade at school. I haven't thought much further ahead than that. What about you?"

She looked suddenly sad, in that familiar way. "I'd like to hear from your father again," she said.

"Do we need money? I can see if the Parmers want me to work more than two days a week."

She shook her head. "No, I'd like more than money from him. I'd just like—someday—to see him."

I was fairly certain this was never going to happen. In fact, if we hadn't received funds from him from time to time, I would have been convinced he was dead. I rarely thought about him anymore. I certainly wouldn't have put his appearance on my list of desires. "Well, it's Wintermoon," I said, lifting my cider glass again. "Maybe your wish will come true."

We sang seasonal carols while doing the dishes, and then my mother yawned. "Goodness, Kellen, I'm too tired to stay up till midnight," she said. "Are you going to? Will you look out the window and watch the neighbors' bonfires?"

"I might even step outside to see them better," I said, to still her fears if she happened to wake and find me out of my bed.

45

She kissed me on the cheek. "Good night, then. Warm Wintermoon wishes."

During the hour that I waited for her to fall asleep, I sorted through her embroidery basket and her rag pile, finding all sorts of treasures. Scraps of lace, snippets of thread, mismatched buttons, and patches of discarded clothing all made their way into my bundle. When I had everything I thought I might need, I checked my mother's bedroom, and she was sound asleep. Pulling on my coat and boots, I headed out into the frosty night.

The full moon was high overhead, an unblinking watchful eye. Stars were suspended in the black sky like raindrops too crystalline to fall. Every breath I inhaled was scented with snow. I hurried through the streets of Thrush Hollow, catching echoes of talk and laughter, glimpsing light and shadows playing around the bonfires in so many neighbors' back yards. The whole world was celebrating Wintermoon.

Certainly much of the world seemed to be celebrating at the tavern, for noise and light spilled out from the front door all the way into the street. I was not used to being this far from home once the sun had gone down, and I was not entirely comfortable as I skirted the front of the building and headed to the back. The laughter inside seemed overloud; the smell of beer and spilled wine was very strong. This was a place for adults, and I was sure I did not belong.

But I had spent much of my life trying to make myself fit in.

The back door was unlocked, and no one was watching the hallway. I crept upstairs, clutching my bag, and was relieved to find Gryffin's door already open. He was seated on a rug before the fire, both canes leaning against the wall. He smiled widely when he saw me.

"I wasn't sure you would come!" he said in a low voice.

"I told you I would," I replied in what was almost a whisper. Even though it was impossible that anyone from the noisy tavern would overhear us, we both had the sense that we were embarked on an illicit adventure, and the more caution we employed, the higher our odds of success. Nonetheless, I could see by the excitement in his face that Gryffin was as delighted with the night's possibilities as I was.

"Show me what you've brought," he commanded, and I dumped the bag of treasures at his feet.

We spent the next hour sorting through the hodgepodge and deciding what we could bend to our uses. First we twined a wreath from the muddle of branches I had found. Holly, of course, always stood for joy, any kind of evergreen for reliability, oak for strength. We lashed them all together with a length of emerald ribbon, which Gryffin said would represent hope, because hope was always green. Then we tied on all the other little bits, and began to endow them with ever more outlandish characteristics.

Gryffin had torn a page from an old book, first assuring me that half the rest of the book was already missing. "This stands for knowledge," he said, and wrapped it around the wreath.

I added a bow of red yarn. "This stands for warmth. You know, like a warm sweater."

47

"This button will represent a shield. It's a miniature shield. It will keep us from harm."

"A toy boat for travel."

"A bird feather for mobility."

"A rose thorn for strength!"

"An acorn for plenty!"

And on this way, giggling our way toward midnight. By the time we were done, we had a very small wreath—barely big enough to rest on my head like a crown—dangling with a colorful assortment of wishes.

"Poke the fire a little; make sure it's really burning," I suggested.

Gryffin shook his head. "Let's go outside. Let's burn our wreath in the back yard, so the smoke goes straight up to the moon."

I was concerned. "It's cold out. And there's still snow everywhere. I don't want you to fall."

"I'll stand just outside the back door," he promised. "I want to see a Wintermoon wreath burn against the night sky."

"It's almost midnight," I said. "Let's go downstairs."

I carried the wreath like a large bracelet over one arm; in the other hand, I held a torch sifted from the fire. Gryffin came behind me, navigating the stairwell with his canes. We could hear the noise of the tavern swelling even more loudly as the clocks ticked closer to the magical hour. The small sounds of our passage were wholly drowned out by the yelling and cheering down the hall.

I helped Gryffin across the threshold and out into the

bitterly cold night. He gasped, then smiled, and took a firmer grip on his canes as he planted them in the snow. Behind us, a wild yell from the tavern indicated that laggard midnight had finally arrived.

"Do it now," Gryffin said, and I touched the brand to the wreath. The greenery was slow to catch on fire, but the drier scraps of wood and cloth instantly danced with flame. I slid the torch through the circlet of fire, holding the safe end of wood in my ungloved hand, and watched them both burn. Orange and yellow and red against the white and black of the snowy night.

Finally the wreath was blazing so fiercely that its shape was hard to distinguish, and then it fell apart completely, landing with a hiss in the snow. I tossed my burning branch down beside it, and both of them continued to smolder for another five minutes, till the wetness of the snow and the disintegration of the fuel put them out. Black cinders flickered against the whiteness of the snowbank, and the scent of spruce circled us on a lazy drift of smoke.

"Warm Wintermoon to you, Kellen," Gryffin whispered. "May everything you wished for come true."

Winter wound its way through the season as if each month was a maze of hedges, too overgrown to navigate with speed. The air always felt heavy, the sky on the verge of darkness. It was dreary and cold, with very few moments of brightness. I felt as if I trudged through the season.

The weather was bad enough so often that Gryffin missed a great deal of school, and consequently, we fell out of the habit of going to the Parmers' house on a regular basis. Sarah still invited us over from time to time, and I would work while Gryffin and Sarah studied, but the visits were rare and seemed too short.

I was needed at home more, anyway. My mother had decided that one way to supplement her income would be to take in travelers, and so she had worked out an arrangement with the local inn that she would accommodate visitors whenever their own rooms were full. She also discreetly advertised this service with a small sign set in the parlor window, and we often caught the attention of customers who did not want to pay the prices the innkeeper charged. So, in a typical week, we might have four days when strangers slept at our house. Naturally, they all required fresh bedding and tolerable meals, as well as a fire in the grate, so there was much more work to do around the house.

The new enterprise also required us to rethink our own sleeping arrangements, for the house was small and boasted only two bedrooms. Guests were accommodated in the one that used to be mine, which meant I needed somewhere else to store my clothes—and somewhere else to sleep. At first I brought an uncomfortable cot into my mother's room and set it up at the foot of her bed, but I found her dreams troublesome. She spoke often during the night, pleadingly and with great urgency, and now and then she cried out. Questioned in the morning, she could never recall what pictures had stalked her sleep, but listening to her in the dark made me sad and uneasy. Consequently, I looked for another bed. I tried the parlor sofa, but it was too soft; I tried the attic, but it was too cold and full of spiders. Eventually I settled on the kitchen floor, next to the stove as it cooled, and I found this both comfortable and somehow comforting.

Naturally, a young girl couldn't be sleeping out in the open when there were strangers in the house, particularly when they were men, so it became even more essential that I be presented as male. Paying customers, I soon learned, cared very little who cleaned their rooms or brought in the wood for their fires; they just wanted prompt and uncomplaining service. If I was anonymous and efficient, I was invisible, and this suited me fine. I did my work, said very little, and appreciated the additional money that came in.

I had less time for schoolwork and less time for Gryffin, but I managed to combine them as often as possible. That is, when I had missed a few days of school and was hopelessly behind in my lessons, I would spend an afternoon in the room above the tavern, and Gryffin would tutor me as he had tutored Sarah Parmer. I made enough progress to graduate to the middle grade by the time the school year ended. Mr. Shelby was proud of me, and my mother celebrated by buying me a new pair of shoes. They were boxy and thick, suitable to wear while tramping through deep woods or dirty city streets, and I loved them.

Gryffin gave me a ribbon, scarlet and shiny. I laughed and threaded it through my hair, where the red made a vivid contrast against the black. "Where did you get *this*?" I asked. "You haven't even left the house for days, as far as I know." The snow had finally retreated, now that spring at last was here, but rain had kept inside everyone who didn't have urgent business.

He smiled. "Peddler man was downstairs having a drink a few days ago. I was in the kitchen, helping my aunt Dora, and he came in to see if she wanted to buy any of his goods. When he got out the buttons and ribbons, I saw this."

"I don't know that I'll ever have a chance to wear it," I said.

He was still smiling. "You're wearing it now."

"What were you doing to help your aunt?"

"She likes to have me work in the kitchen sometimes. I sit at the table and chop vegetables, or mix bread. As long as she brings me whatever I need to work with, I can do a lot." He extended one hand and made fist. "My arms are strong," he said. "I can work with my hands all day."

"You should make your uncle pay you."

He made a face. "I think he thinks this is how I earn my keep."

"So you'll be working in the kitchen all summer?"

"Some of the time. Mr. Shelby is having summer classes for some of the students who need to make up missed work. I'm going to study with him until I catch up. And I'll help him tutor some of the smaller children. He said he could pay me a little for that, so my uncle was happy with the idea."

"You'll be busy," I commented.

"Not too busy," he said. "Not when you have time to come by."

I found, despite all the inconveniences, that I rather liked to have company at our house. It made a nice change from my mother's madness and my own solitude. Some of the guests were taciturn and ill-tempered; others were quiet and kept to themselves. But a few were outgoing and talkative, and over meals would describe their adventures on the road. One young man, traveling between Merendon and Movington, told us of the great ships he had sailed on and the fabulous foreign cities he had visited. I would not have believed him, except that he carried exotic jewels in his saddlebags, which he showed me after dinner. Before he left in the morning, he gave me a small gift, a coral-colored disk carved with such an intricate design that my fingers could not resist tracing the patterns over and over in the smooth stone. While my mother was out of the room he told me that it was an ancient symbol for femininity.

"In a few years, find yourself a girl, and give her that, hey?" he said, winking at me. "It'll make her fond of you, if you catch my meaning."

"Maybe you should keep it for yourself," I said, rather unwillingly. My hands already loved the smooth feel of the stone, the complex text of the indentations.

He waved his hand. "Brought twenty of them back with me. I'll sell a few in Wodenderry. Keep a few for myself, too." He laughed.

"Thank you, then."

He winked again. "Don't tell your mama."

My mother was unhappy enough with him without that provocation, for it turned out he had departed without paying his shot. On the other hand, he had left on her pillow a short necklace of tumbled onyx beads, which even I knew she could sell for enough money to cover one night's lodging. She didn't sell it, though. She kept it and, now and then, she wore it, always looking both embarrassed that she loved such a simple thing so much, and pleased that it was actually hers.

I never showed her my own rusty red prize. But sometimes I slept with it under my pillow, and on those nights my dreams were different.

Chapter Six

Summermoon came, and a certain amount of turmoil with it.

The town was full, because Summermoon was that kind of festival. Farmers from outlying acres came to town; cousins dropped by to visit their families; anyone with any product to sell crowded into the central square. Thrush Hollow had always had a Summermoon Fair—small, of course, by the standards of bigger towns, but plenty festive for us—and this year was no different. So there was a sprawling marketplace of peddlers and merchants set up on the edge of town, and there were musicians hired to play on the street corners. Everyone who owned an inn, a tavern, or an eating establishment bought extra provisions and hired additional help against the onslaught of customers.

My mother was excited because she had figured out a way to make extra money during the holiday. She would raise her prices a little on the bedroom, and she would rent out the parlor couch for someone who wasn't too particular about privacy or comfort. Meals usually came with the accommodations, but for this one week of the year, she would charge for them separately. Thus she could, in a few days' time, make almost as much as she made during an ordinary month.

The bedroom was claimed almost immediately by a young couple who had not been married long. She was starting to swell with what she informed us was her first pregnancy, and they had decided to come to town for Summermoon this year since they weren't sure they'd have the energy for it next year, what with the baby and the farm and all. The day before Summermoon, the sofa was let to a slightly tattered older man who announced he did magic tricks. He was going to set up a booth in the marketplace and dazzle all the fairgoers with sleight of hand. Over dinner he gave us a preview, making spoons disappear and pulling a coin out of the pregnant woman's ear. He also did a little juggling and was able to balance a knife on the edge of his forefinger for an amazingly long period of time. If I had had a few spare coppers, I would have thrown one to him. As it was, I gave him an extra helping of pie after the meal.

At dawn on Summermoon itself, a third stranger appeared at our door, asking for a place to stay.

My mother and I were already up and working in the kitchen, preparing breakfast for our three guests. We both were startled to hear a gentle rapping at the back door, accompanied by a soft voice. "Hello? I knocked at the front, but no one answered."

I wiped my hands on my shirt and opened the door, and a man stepped inside. He was of middle height and rather boxy build, with short dark hair and a rather dreamy expression. For a moment I thought he might be as young as the newlywed couple now sleeping in my bedroom. Then the sunlight fell oddly on his cheeks, and I thought he might be my mother's age. Then he smiled down at me, and again I was unsure. But there was something inviting in his expression. It was impossible not to smile back.

"Hello," he said again. "I'm glad I didn't wake you. After no one answered my first knock, I thought maybe it was too early to try. But I've traveled most of the night and I desperately need some sleep."

My mother patted the flour from her hands and looked dismayed. "I don't think we have a place to put you," she said. I could tell she was trying to figure out a way to make that sentence false. "There's even someone sleeping in the parlor."

He sighed, then smiled again. "And the inn is full, and so is the residence up at the edge of the town, where someone already directed me."

"The Parmer house?" I asked. They had been known to take in travelers now and then. Thrush Hollow must be even more crowded than I'd thought if the Parmers didn't have any spare room.

He nodded. "I believe that's what it was called. I left my horse and cart with them, but they had no place for me. Several people recommended I try the Carmichaels. That's you, I believe." My mother and I both nodded. He continued in a coaxing voice, "I don't require much, really. A place to lie down. A mat in the hallway. I promise that I'm quiet and easygoing."

My mother bit her lip. "I wish we could accommodate you."

"Will you sleep on the floor in the kitchen?" I asked him. My mother shot me a look of surprise that modulated to hopeful calculation.

"Gladly," said the stranger.

I nodded. "Mother, I'll stay in your room. We'll let him sleep here." I gave him a warning look. "We're up early, starting the bread. You can't expect to sleep late."

"I will rise happily when you do." He glanced around, his expression dimming a little. "Though I can see that I will have to wait till nightfall before I can rest, since you are obviously busy in the middle of my bedchamber."

"Let me make up a place in my room," my mother said. "If you don't mind the floor. Sleep as long as you like."

"You are very good," he said gratefully. "I'm ready to drop."

"Where are your bags?" my mother asked.

"On the front porch."

"Kellen, you fetch his things," my mother directed. "You, sir, give me a few moments to freshen the room. You may sit here in the kitchen while you wait. Are you hungry? There's fresh bread and some nice jam."

"Famished," he said, sinking to one of the sturdy chairs around the kitchen table. "But please call me by my name. I'm Ayler."

"Why are you in Thrush Hollow, Ayler?" I heard my mother ask as I ducked out of the door. His voice was lost to me as I darted around the house, but I thought I heard him mention the Summermoon Fair. It would be the reason anyone came to Thrush Hollow at this time of year.

Two rather dilapidated bags huddled where they'd been dropped before the front door. They were much patched and of a drab olive color. Looped around one worn handle was a leather thong attached to a hollow wooden ball. It was cut and pierced so you could see little wooden chips inside. Absently, to hear it rattle, I lifted the ball and shook it, but it produced no sound. I shook it again, harder, watching the chips fling themselves against the ball's curved interior. Still silent. The wood was so soft, or so strange, that it was incapable of making a sound.

I felt a tickle in my stomach as I examined the sphere more intently. The light stain of the finish did little to hide the close grain of the wood, and I was fairly certain that I held a toy made from the trunk of a kirrenberry tree.

A Safe-Keeper had come to Thrush Hollow and was staying at my mother's house.

When I returned to the kitchen, Ayler was still sitting at the table, eating bread and jam with great satisfaction. My mother had disappeared, no doubt back in her own room making the bed and arranging a pallet on the floor. I heard a few muffled bumps and curses from the parlor, so I knew the magician was up and moving about and would soon be in the kitchen looking for food. Not much time to talk.

I set Ayler's bags down in front of him and pointed at the ball. He smiled at me, the dreaminess of his expression very pronounced.

"You're a Safe-Keeper," I said.

He nodded and swallowed. "Do you have any secrets you wish to confide?"

"No. But if I did, I could tell you and you would never repeat them to anyone, *ever*, and you would die and they would still be secrets."

He considered this as he cut himself another piece of bread. "Sometimes secrets only need to be kept for a time," he said. "Sometimes my role is to protect them until they are strong enough to stand on their own."

"If I told you a secret, I would never want you to repeat it."

He nodded. "And some secrets will go with me to my grave."

"I'm a girl," I said, all in rush. I was a little surprised to hear myself say the words. I had not bothered to give this information to any of our other guests, and there was no reason Ayler needed to know it.

"And is that a secret?" he asked gravely.

"Not exactly. Some people know it, some people don't. My mother wishes I was a boy." Before he could speak again, I added dryly, "That's not a secret, either."

"And what do you wish you were?" he asked.

I had never actually thought about it that way before. "I wish I was a girl who could do whatever she wanted," I said at last.

He swallowed another piece of bread. "And isn't that what you are?"

I had never actually thought about *that*, either. "Maybe," I said, my voice uncertain. "But there are days I don't like who I have to be."

"There are days all of us don't like who we are," Ayler replied serenely. "And there are days we work to become people we like better."

I came a step closer. "What would happen," I asked, "if I told you a secret that wasn't true? Would you know?"

He shook his head. "I'm no Truth-Teller. I am not blessed with the ability to recognize a lie."

"But then, if I told you something false?" I persisted.

He laughed. "Then I would forever keep a lie in my store of secrets."

"I wonder if anybody ever has," I mused.

"In my experience," he said, "when someone is desperate enough to seek a Safe-Keeper, what he has to say is true. Or he believes it to be true. Or it becomes true. It is the dreadful truths that needed to be shielded. The dreadful lies may run about in the sunshine all day long and no one will care."

"Some things are dreadful even when they're not secrets," I said.

Ayler nodded. "This is also true."

My mother came bustling back in. She was glowing with the happiness of good fortune. Another paying guest! Such luck! "The room is ready anytime you want to go back and sleep," she said. "Let me know when you'd like me to wake you."

Ayler rose to his feet, then bent to retrieve his bags. "If I'm not up wandering about by mid-afternoon, I would consider it a kindness if you would call for me," he said. "Thank you so much for your hospitality." He nodded in my direction. "I have enjoyed my brief conversation with your son."

My mother glowed briefly brighter. "I don't know what I'd do without him."

She guided him back to her room while I resumed my work in the kitchen. I was smiling.

But the day held some ugliness. I was returning from the market fair, having bought dried spices there for my mother, when behind me I heard running footsteps and a sudden shout. I spun around, not quickly enough, and was instantly in the middle of a nasty little brawl. There was Carlon, of course, and two of his friends from school. Maybe they'd gotten hold of some Summermoon wine and were feeling more than ordinarily boisterous. Maybe they had been lying in wait for me; maybe they were just roaming the streets of Thrush Hollow, looking for distractions. In any case, I was not a match for all three of them. I was soon a mass of pain and bruises where I had dropped to the ground, curled in a ball to shield myself from the worst of the kicks and blows. The spices were lost somewhere in the scuffle, trampled into the grass and mud.

The fight didn't last all that long. It was Summermoon, and the streets were crowded, and I heard a man's voice shouting out. "You boys! Stop that! Get along, now, and don't cause trouble." Carlon gave me a last quick kick in the ribs, then they all laughed and ran down the street. My rescuer came a few steps closer.

"Are you badly hurt, son?"

"I don't think so," I said, slowly pushing myself to a sitting position. Nothing was broken, anyway, though I was a mess of blood and dirt. I rose to my feet a little shakily. "Some cuts and bruises, I guess."

"Well, go on home, now, and try to stay out of fights," he advised me. His good deed done, he turned and hurried off to the fair.

More slowly, I went on my way. My face hurt and my lip burned, and I could taste blood in my mouth. The worst was my right leg, which was painful to walk on. But I imagined how much harder it must be for Gryffin, and I gritted my teeth and kept moving.

My mother exclaimed with dismay when she saw me, and sent me out to the back to wash up. I dumped two buckets of water over my head—my thrifty idea of cleaning my face and my clothes at the same time—and washed the dirt off my face. I would live, I decided.

Fortunately for me, the young couple had headed for the fair a few hours ago, so I could step into my room and rummage through my dresser for fresh clothes. In a few moments, I was clean, I had combed back my wet hair, and I had dabbed ointment onto all the cuts that looked worst. Best I could do.

When I returned to the kitchen, my mother was gone, and Ayler was sitting at the table eating a late lunch.

"What happened to you?" he asked, laying aside his fork.

"It's a secret," I said sourly.

He laughed, but his face was compassionate. "Someone doesn't like you much."

I shrugged. "Bullies from the schoolhouse. Where's my mother?"

"Off to the fair to get spices, she said."

I nodded. Obviously, she was replacing the ones I'd lost. "Anything else you need?" I asked politely.

He shook his head. "If you want," he said, "I can show you how to fight back."

I was skeptical. "Against three boys?"

He gave me that dreamer's smile. "I didn't say you'd win."

I looked him over. He wasn't tall, but he was strongly built—probably some muscle hidden under his baggy trousers and loose shirt. "You really know how to fight?"

He nodded solemnly. "I know the secret methods taught to the soldiers in the royal guard of the faraway kingdom of Foltavi." I laughed. He smiled and continued, "I also know the basics of boxing. And a few tricks I can show you. It might even up the odds a bit."

"All right," I said. "Let me clean up the kitchen first."

Chapter Seven

he Safe-Keeper and I spent an hour in the back yard while he demonstrated how to make and land a fist, where to strike an opponent, and how to protect myself if I did go down. I was not in the best of shape due to my recent escapade, but I liked the lessons well enough to promise to practice when I had a chance.

"You're strong—that's to your advantage," Ayler said. "I haven't met too many girls with that kind of power in their arms."

I balled my hand and curled my arm in a boastful pose. "Chopping wood," I said.

"And you're smart," he said. "You'll find that gives you the ability to fight in entirely different ways."

I shook my head. "Not smart like Gryffin."

"Who's that?"

"My friend."

"Maybe you can spar with him. Would he want to come over and learn some of my secret boxing tricks?"

"He can't. His legs are bad. He has trouble walking."

"No, then, not a boxer, I suppose," Ayler said.

"He wants to go to Wodenderry and study law or accounting," I said.

"I've been to Wodenderry many times," Ayler said. "It's a wonderful city! Full of trouble and beauty. You might like it yourself."

I sighed. We had paused after our exertions to drink about three glasses of water each, for it was midday and hot. I reflected that my second set of clothes had now gotten almost as dirty as the first set. So I dumped water over my head again to help cool me down. Ayler did the same.

"I doubt I'll ever go to Wodenderry," I said. "I've never been anywhere."

"Not even Merendon? Or Lowford? Or Tambleham?" he asked, naming the closest major towns.

"Never. Well, I was born in Tambleham, but I was only two days old when they brought me here, and I've never left since." I glanced up at him as he was wiping water from his eyes. "I suppose you've been everywhere?"

He nodded. "I'm an itinerant. I never stay still." He smiled down at me. "Most Safe-Keepers find themselves a little cottage in some town, and plant their kirrenberry trees, and sit and wait for secrets to come to their doorsteps. I always thought it was more interesting to go looking for secrets. And then I carry them safely with me when I go."

"There hasn't been a Safe-Keeper living in Thrush Hollow since I was born."

He smiled. "Then I'll have to come back more often."

I considered. "I wonder if Gryffin has any secrets."

"Let's go ask him."

Gryffin was seated in the kitchen, his fingers flying as he chopped onions and grated carrots and split celery. His aunt shot us a harassed look as we came in, for she was attempting to stir a pot on the stove and check a dish in the oven while scolding a weeping young barmaid at the same time.

"What do you want, Kellen?" she demanded. "We're all too busy to talk right now."

"Can't Gryffin come out just for a few minutes? I wanted him to talk with the Safe-Keeper."

Dora's sharp eyes grew even sharper as she took in Ayler's round face and abstracted expression. "That's a Safe-Keeper?" she said in a slow voice. "What would he be doing in Thrush Hollow?"

"Collecting secrets," Ayler said amiably. "If you have any to share."

"I don't have secrets," she snapped. "Everyone knows my business."

"Then you have an easier life than many people," Ayler said.

"I'll come out for a few minutes," Gryffin said, drying his hands on the front of his shirt and reaching for his canes. "Just to say hello."

The heat outside was bearable if we sat in the shade the tavern threw over the back lawn. The kitchen garden was full of stalks and vines greedily soaking up sun; I could smell the pungent leaves of tomato plants and spot telltale signs of red and yellow on some of the ripening gourds. The bench beside the house was only long enough to accommodate two people, so I let Gryffin and Ayler have it while I settled to the ground before them.

"If you want to confide something in me," Ayler said, his voice grave but his eyes twinkling, "we'd best be sending Kellen on her way."

"She knows everything I might say to you," Gryffin replied. Then he cut his eyes back toward Ayler. "You know she's a girl?"

"People tend to tell me things."

Gryffin leaned forward. "Here's my secret wish," he said. "I wish Kellen would come with me when I go to Wodenderry. I wish she would leave her mother's house and go where she's treated better."

"How odd," I said, "when you are not treated well yourself."

"Yes, but I'll be leaving." Gryffin appealed to the Safe-Keeper. "I wish she was somewhere that she could live like a girl, and people wouldn't think she was strange, and she could be happy." He had never said this to me before. It seemed that Ayler's presence did indeed induce people to expose their most hidden thoughts.

"I think you've confused me with the Dream-Maker," Ayler said gently. "I have no power to make wishes come true. Merely to hear what you hold in your heart, so that things too heavy to bear alone are shared."

Gryffin turned his head away. "I think it is my dreams

that are too heavy to bear," he said in a muffled voice. "I think it is my dreams I cannot speak out loud."

I had an inspiration. "You must know the Dream-Maker," I said to Ayler. "Next time you're in Wodenderry, seek her out. Tell her to come to Thrush Hollow, for there are all sorts of dreams here that need to come true."

"I do know Melinda, who is a lovely woman," Ayler replied with a smile. "But these days she travels much less than she used to. She is more than seventy now, and I think she is growing tired."

"Well, tell her not to be too tired till she comes to Thrush Hollow," I said.

Ayler nodded as if accepting a commission. "I will send her on her way."

When Ayler learned that Gryffin had never been to a Summermoon Festival, because it was too difficult for him to navigate both the crowds and the distance, he was determined to rectify the omission. "Can you ride?" he asked.

Gryffin and I both stared at him. "Ride a *horse*?" Gryffin repeated. "No."

"Well, you could sit on one, couldn't you?" Ayler said. "My little mare is very docile. I put children on her back all the time. I think she'll carry you as long as my hand is on the bridle."

"And if she bolts while Gryffin is on her back?" I demanded.

Ayler grinned. "That at least won't happen. Gryffin may tire, for it is not so easy as it looks to sit on a horse, but then we will take him aside and let him sprawl on the grass awhile. I'll bring a blanket. I think this will not be so difficult to do."

Gryffin was trying hard not to look excited. "I would like to try," he said casually. "If it's not too much trouble."

Ayler smiled. "I think it must be why I felt compelled to come to Thrush Hollow."

We scattered for a time, Gryffin returning to the kitchen to finish his chores, me returning to my own house on the same errand, and Ayler off to canvass the town for secrets. We all met at the tavern again in three hours, just as the sun was finally sinking enough to abate some of the high heat of the afternoon. The Safe-Keeper was leading his horse, a rather squat black mare with a diamond-shaped white mark on her face and eyes as dreamy as Ayler's own.

"I borrowed a saddle from Josh Parmer," Ayler said. "We can adjust the stirrups till they feel right for your legs."

The little mare showed amazing patience as Ayler lifted Gyffin into the saddle and went to some trouble to make him comfortable. I could tell that my friend still felt noticeable pain in the unfamiliar position, but his face was so creased with delight that it was obvious he considered the trade-off worth it. He looked down at the two of us and laughed out loud.

"I feel so tall!" he exclaimed. "This is great fun!"

"Let's see how it feels once you're in motion," Ayler said, and gently tugged on the horse's bridle. The mare obediently stepped forward. Gryffin whooped and grabbed the saddle horn, but he stayed on. Ayler continued to lead the horse toward the fair.

"I'll bring your canes," I called to Gryffin. "Just in case
you need them."

So we made an odd procession as we slowly moved
through the streets of Thrush Hollow, the man leading the
horse with the boy in the saddle, me behind them with the
canes slung over my shoulder. Every once in a while I would
hear Ayler ask a question; every once in a while I would
hear Gyffin laugh for what appeared to be no reason at all.

The streets were fairly empty, as most people were
already at the fair. I was not sure how Ayler intended to
negotiate the narrow, crowded aisles between the close-set
booths, but it was soon clear that was not his plan.

"We'll walk around the perimeter," he said, for the
booths lining the four sides of the fair had their tables
turned outward. "That will at least give you a taste of what's
available. Then perhaps Kellen will run quickly through the
inner booths and report back to us what might be for sale
that you would be interested in purchasing, so you don't
have to miss any possible treasures."

"I don't have much money with me," Gryffin said.

"You won't need much," Ayler assured him. "Everything
is cheap at the fair."

And indeed, he was right. Merchants were selling everything from shoes to gloves to shirts to bows to beads to pot-
tery to cakes and breads and fruits and ales, and all of it at
very reasonable prices. Moving still with that careful slow-
ness, we circled the whole fair once, so Gryffin could
observe what choices were available to him and decide
where to spend his limited funds. I made a quick foray

through the hot and densely packed booths and came back to describe what riches could be found in the areas denied to Gryffin. We decided, recklessly, that only the most accessible booths deserved our patronage, so we made a strange but satisfying meal from an assortment of vegetable skewers, cheese rounds, and exotic eggs, hard-boiled and edible but dropped from no poultry I'd ever come across. None of us wanted the alcohol on sale at so many different venues, but we drank from Ayler's water flask and were just as happy.

There was a bookseller at the very edge of the fair, his booth not quite so crowded as the others, and Gryffin actually asked Ayler to lift him down so he could sort through the merchandise. I handed over the canes, then held the horse's bridle while Ayler stood behind Gryffin to protect him from careless strangers. Gryffin spent his last coppers on a volume that was in such disrepair that the pages were coming free of the binding and much of the leather was flaking off from the cover.

"Folk tales," he said happily as Ayler helped him back on the horse. "I've wanted something like this forever."

It was clear the excursion had tired Gryffin. We stayed perhaps an hour—the sun still had not completely set—before we decided to turn back for town. I walked right beside the horse this time, close enough to catch Gryffin if he started to fall, while Ayler sought the smoothest route home. More than once, Gryffin put his hand out to rest it on my shoulder, and I stiffened my back to take as much of his weight as I could.

The tavern, of course, was alive with revelry when we finally made our way to the back door. But most of the light and noise poured from the front of the building; the back was dark and comparatively quiet.

"Do you need any help getting up to your room?" Ayler inquired. "If not, I'll take my horse back to the Parmers'."

There was just the slightest hesitation from Gryffin. "No. I can make it myself. But I think I'll sit outside awhile and listen to the crickets."

"Kellen? Do you want to walk with me?"

"I'll stay with Gryffin a bit," I decided. "I'll see you at my mother's."

Gryffin and I settled ourselves on the bench and leaned against the house. There was a burst of laughter from the front of the tavern and the sound of something shattering. More laughter. Above us, the moon was full and yellow, yawning with the exertion of enduring a full day of merriment.

"Why don't you want to go upstairs?" I asked after we had been sitting in silence a few moments.

"The room's occupied," he said.

"Who's occupying it? And how can you tell from down here?"

He just looked at me a moment in the faint moonlight. "There were two candles in the window," he said. "A signal that the room's in use."

"In use for—" I began, and then my mouth hung open. "You can't mean—people who are drinking in the tavern want—they go up to use your *bedroom*?"

Gryffin nodded. "Usually just on weekends. And holidays. I spend a lot of time down on this bench."

"Even in winter?" I demanded.

He shrugged. "In winter I usually wait in the kitchen."

I made a little grunting noise. "Kitchen's not so bad. I've slept on the floor in front of our stove a lot of times."

"Easier to get something to eat if you're hungry late at night," he agreed.

"But do people know?" I said. "I mean, I can't think the mayor—and Mr. Shelby—and the Parmers—well, they would be appalled to find out what's going on here at the tavern."

"Obviously some people know," Gyffin said with a ghost of a smile. "But I don't know about all the respectable people. It's not like I'm going to tell them. My uncle Frederick would just hate me even more."

"He couldn't hate *you* as much as I hate *him*," I said instantly.

Now Gryffin laughed out loud. But he said, "I've never found that hate does much good. It's better just to figure out what you can do to get out of the situation."

"Study hard and go to Wodenderry," I said.

"That's my plan."

"Maybe Ayler will help you," I said. "I like him."

"Yes," he said. "I have a feeling Ayler might help us both."

"Although sometimes it seems both of us have too many problems to be fixed by anybody," I said with a little laugh.

"That's what Summermoon is for," said Gryffin. "To convince us to believe in magical possibilities."

Ayler was gone two days after Summermoon, none of our problems resolved. But it did seem that, as was true with so much in my life, events were put in motion during those lush green months. I practiced my boxing skills, finding an unexpected and useful sparring partner in Sarah's youngest brother. The first time I successfully punched Carlon in the nose, drawing a satisfying amount of blood, was the last time he ever attacked me.

Gryffin continued to spend the occasional evening outside on the back bench, or inside on the kitchen floor. I continued to despise his uncle, and to mull over what I might do to make him improve his treatment of my friend.

My mother continued to rent out the parlor sofa as well as my bedroom, bringing more money to the household and more chaos to my life.

And bringing more strangers through our door.

Chapter Eight

hase Beerin arrived late on a blustery fall day and told us he would stay a couple of nights on the sofa in the parlor. He was in his early twenties, with blond-brown hair that had a romantic curl, and brown eyes so dark they could not help but appear brooding. I had turned thirteen at the end of summer and was starting to look more like a girl, especially if I didn't dress in disastrously ill-fitting clothes. I had started to spend time thinking about Sarah's younger brother and two of the boys in class, wondering if they would notice me if I wore frilly dresses and tried to do something about my abysmal hair. I blushed for no reason and laughed at no provocation, at least when I was talking to one of the boys I admired. For the first time in my life, I really, really, *really* wished to be someone other than who I was.

Chase Beerin was the handsomest man I had ever met.

The first night he stayed with us, I honestly didn't think I'd be able to breathe if he looked at me. I was afraid to serve him dinner because I thought I might accidentally touch his hand, and then I would start with mortification, and then I would drop the entire tureen of soup in his lap, and then I would have to die. When he asked me simple questions— about the price of the accommodations, the layout of the town—I turned a hot red and found it difficult to answer.

He acted as if he didn't notice my giddiness and infatuation. Maybe he was just used to such treatment from all the young girls he met; surely everyone must see him as an unparalleled paragon of perfection. Or else he thought I was a girl with mental deficiencies who actually functioned fairly well given that she couldn't put together two coherent thoughts. During the three days he stayed with us, he always treated me with gentle courtesy and never, not even once, said anything that might be construed as flirtatious.

He knew I was a girl, though, and I didn't even have to tell him. Maybe it was because the shabby clothes were not hiding my figure as they should. Maybe because I laughed too much or played with my hair when he was in the room. Maybe because he had trained himself to notice people and their physical conditions.

He was on his way to Wodenderry to study to be a doctor. Thereby adding to his godlike stature in my eyes.

He gave us this information during the second night's dinner, when I had somewhat recovered myself, though I still felt fluttery in his presence. We had a second guest in the house just then, an older woman renting my room. She had stayed with us several times in the past. She was stick-thin and cold-natured, but even she was batting her eyes and smiling at Chase Beerin.

"I think it must be very hard to learn everything you'll have to know to be a doctor," she said, giving him her warmest smile. "What made you decide to pursue such a career?"

"I felt so helpless two years ago when my sister was sick," he replied in his earnest way. "We nursed her back to health, but it took so long, and we were afraid we were going to lose her. I never wanted to feel that useless again in the face of illness."

"Was she very young?" the woman asked sympathetically.

He glanced at me. "About Kellen's age, I would guess. Kellen looks a little like her, too." He smiled briefly. "She's not quite as wild as my sister, though."

The other guest dismissed me with a quick, disbelieving look. "So you've been accepted at the Physicians' College in Wodenderry? You must be very clever."

I was still stunned at the revelations that Chase knew what I was and thought I looked like someone related to him. My mother, handing around the potatoes from the head of the table, frowned briefly at his observation, but decided not to comment. Chase continued to tell us about his family and confided that he was a little nervous about his upcoming medical education.

"For you're right. It will be very hard. But I have always managed to do everything I set out to do, even if I had to try a few times before I succeeded. So I'm determined to do well at doctoring, too. I have actually been studying for the past year with a physician in Merendon—informally, you know, but learning what I could. He said I had great potential and that I could come back and work with him once I've attained my degree."

"And will you?" my mother asked.

"I don't know. I might go back to my hometown instead. Or I might stay in Wodenderry for a few years. I shall have to see how I like the royal city."

After the meal, he asked for directions to the tavern, where he was meeting a friend who had moved to Thrush Hollow.

"I can lead you there," I offered. "I've got to take Gryffin his assignments, anyway."

A few minutes later we were walking through the quiet town—well, I was trying hard not to skip in my excitement at spending a few moments alone with Chase Beerin, but he was strolling along quite casually. Early dark was in the process of stamping out the last of daylight, and the air was cool enough to make a brisk walk advisable.

"So who's Gryffin and why does he need assignments?" Chase asked after we had walked a couple of minutes in silence.

"Oh! He's my friend. He lives above the tavern. He goes to school with me, but he couldn't make it today, so our teacher gave me work to bring him."

"Why couldn't he make it? Was he sick?"

"He has—there's something wrong with his legs," I said. "And sometimes they hurt him so much he can't walk. That's what happened today."

Chase Beerin glanced down at me, and I could see a

professional interest lighting his dark eyes. "What's wrong with them?"

I shrugged. "I don't know. They were twisted when he was born."

"Can I—do you think he would allow me to look at him? I don't know if I could do anything to help him, but it's possible."

I smiled. How could anyone help *adoring* this man? "Let's ask him."

Gryffin, found lounging on his bed surrounded by books and candles, greeted Chase Beerin's offer with polite doubt. "I've been like this a long time," he said. "I don't know that anyone can help me."

"Maybe not," he said, "What have others done for you?"

"I don't know if my mother called in anyone when I was a baby," Gryffin said carefully. "But I haven't had a chance to consult a doctor since I've lived in Thrush Hollow."

I thought I saw a good deal of comprehension in Chase's eyes, but he merely nodded. "Kellen, you might want to leave the room," he said. "I'm going to ask Gryffin to take off his trousers."

"I don't mind seeing his legs if Gryffin doesn't mind my seeing them," I said.

Chase laughed. "That wasn't exactly what I was worried about."

Gryffin was grinning, too. "Kellen can stay if she wants," he said. "I'll keep on my underthings."

Now I was blushing *furiously*, because it had never exactly occurred to me to think about Gryffin being a boy. I mean, he was, of course, but in the same sort of way that I was a girl—a way that no one particularly noticed. "I just thought maybe I'd be able to do something to help," I said in a strangled voice.

"And so you might," Chase said. "Do you suppose there's any kind of ointment or salve in the house? I have some with me, but it's in my bag back at Kellen's."

"In the kitchen cupboard," Gryffin said. "My aunt puts it on her hands after she's done all the washing."

"Perhaps Kellen can bring us some," Chase said.

I flew down to the kitchen, where fortunately not even Dora was stationed at the moment, found a can of herb-scented cream, and ran up the stairs again. By this time, Gryffin's trousers had been removed and he lay barefoot and half-naked on the bed. His legs were so thin, so white, and so frail-looking that for a moment I was speechless. They were also twisted and marred with great, painful-looking lumps, and I saw places that looked purple as from permanent bruises. I wanted to cry.

I didn't. "Here's the cream," I said.

Chase nodded. "Good. Can you set it in the fire for a little while, so that it heats up? Not too hot. Stir it with your finger, and bring it to me when it feels warm to your skin."

While I did this, Chase sat at the edge of the bed and began to methodically straighten Gryffin's legs. Once in a while I heard Gryffin gasp with pain, and several times I heard Chase ask, "Did that hurt? How about this? Does this hurt?" Most often the answer was yes, but sometimes it was no. I thought Gryffin sounded breathless, as if the pain was too great to allow him to take in much air.

Soon enough I carried the can of salve back to Chase. He scooped out a big glob and rolled it between his hands, then spread it on both of Gryffin's legs from his toes to his swollen knees.

"Have you ever had a massage? No?" Chase asked. "I'm going to see if that helps a little. Sometimes it relaxes the muscles and makes the spasms go away. Let me know if any of this is painful. It's not supposed to be."

And he slowly and methodically began to rub the cream into Gryffin's malformed legs. I saw Gryffin's hands clench and then relax, and the tense expression on his face eased as well. "No, that doesn't hurt," he said in a wondering voice. "In fact, it feels good."

"Good," Chase said.

I crowded as close to the bed as I could, watching how Chase placed his hands, where he applied pressure, where he did not. "Could I learn to do that?" I asked.

Chase glanced up at me. "Probably. It takes some strength to do it right, though."

"My hands are very strong," I assured him.

Chase shifted. "Then sit down here a minute." I brought over the battered ottoman and perched on the edge. "Put some cream on your hands. Now place them—like this—on Gryffin's leg and exert a little pressure. . . ."

Under my fingertips, Gryffin's skin felt oily with lotion, but thin as paper. I was afraid cause it to split and tear. Beneath the insufficient flesh lay the knotted muscles and the fragile bones, just as likely to fray and break. I was used to doing hard work but nothing this delicate, nothing freighted with so much consequence. I looked up from my hands and saw Gryffin watching me.

"I don't want to hurt you," I whispered.

He shook his head. "I don't think you can."

"A little more pressure, Kellen," Chase directed. "Now move your hands—like this—yes. . . ."

We worked on him for about an hour, by which time I was exhausted and Gryffin had relaxed into a sort of blissful silence, head thrown back, eyes closed. Not until Chase nodded at me and we both lifted our hands did Gryffin open his eyes again.

"That was wonderful," he said. "I feel like I could get up and dance."

"Better not," Chase advised. He smiled and cleaned his hands with a cloth pulled from his back pocket. I was just wiping mine on the front of my shirt. "But I think you'll find that your legs feel stronger in the morning. Walking will be easier." He glanced at me. "If you could get a massage like that once a week, I think you might even make a little progress. And the more you use your legs, the better they'll function. I don't know that you'll ever improve to the point where you don't have to use your canes, but walking will become easier, perhaps."

"Once a week? I can do that," I said.

"Or perhaps your mother or father? You mentioned an aunt—"

"No," Gryffin and I said in unison.

"Well, then. Kellen, if she can." Chase smiled at me and

stood up. "And now I suppose I'd better go hunt up my friend. He'll be wondering what's kept me."

I made a face. "And I'd better get home. My mother will be looking for me. Gryffin, I brought your books and some notes from Mr. Shelby. I'll come by in the morning to get you."

"I'll be waiting."

Chase and I felt our way down the dark stairway and emerged into the chilly night. My hands smelled like flowers and bark and whatever other scents had been stirred into the lotion. My original plan had been to return the salve to the kitchen, until I realized that I would be needing it in the future when I tended to Gryffin. I figured Dora could blame some barmaid or her own carelessness for the disappearance of the container.

"Can you find your way back to my mother's house?" I asked.

Chase nodded. "I'll be back late, though. Don't wait up."

I grinned. "Don't be surprised if I wake you up in the morning when I start breakfast. Even if I don't mean to."

"And don't *you* be surprised if even the promise of a meal isn't enough to get me off of the sofa."

I smiled and half turned to go. Chase had taken a step toward the front of the building when I spoke again. "Thank you," I said. "That was so—Gryffin always has so much pain. That you can take it away like that—it's almost like magic."

Chase shrugged in the dark. "Kindness is a form of magic," he said. "So everyone should be capable of at least a little. Good night. See you in the morning." And he nodded to me and strode off.

I stood there another moment, struck dumb.

Kindness is a form of magic.

Then magic had sprinkled itself across me many times, when I had not even noticed its fey sparkle. I had been used to thinking of my life as bleak and full of darkness, but for the first time it occurred to me how often a stranger had stepped forward to offer me comfort and assistance, no matter how briefly. Ian Shelby. Sarah Parmer. Ayler the Safe-Keeper. The man who had stopped Carlon from beating me in the streets. Chase Beerin. They had been kind to me; most had, in different ways, been kind to Gryffin as well. Looked at that way, my life was a weave of brightness laid over a trembling black, a scrap of midnight velvet spangled with many jewels.

I had another thought as I stood there, trying desperately to understand a completely altered view of my existence. Someday *I* might be the one to offer kindness to someone else in grim and dire circumstances. Someday *I* might be the one with wealth or knowledge or strength or power that could be used to alleviate another person's distress. Such a thought had literally never crossed my mind before. More than once I had been saved. Someday I might save someone else in return.

I considered these ideas as I walked very slowly back to my mother's house, my head down against the searching wind. I thought them over as I lay in front of the stove, soaking up whatever warmth was offered by its dying heat. I wanted to discuss them with Chase Beerin the next morning but, true to his warning, he did not rise for breakfast. He was still sleeping when I left to collect Gryffin on the way to school. When I got home that afternoon, he had already left town.

I never saw Chase Beerin in Thrush Hollow again.

Chapter Nine

Wintermoon came, just as cold as the year before but far less snowy. This time as we stood behind the tavern, torching our own private wreath, Gryffin and I smeared some of the oak branches with a scented cream that I had bought from a recent overnight guest who peddled all sorts of interesting items. It had a fine consistency that pleased Gryffin and turned even my work-roughened hands soft. We had made a point of following Chase's regimen of a weekly massage, and Gryffin was delighted to notice some improvement in his balance, his mobility, and his level of pain. He had missed no school days this entire season because of his legs.

"I think Chase was wrong," Gryffin said. "I think I'll walk without my canes someday after all." To further the attainment of this desire, he had carved miniature versions of them from sticks of wood, and tied them to the wreath to burn.

I had added my own special items to this year's wreath—a scrap of white lace, a length of red ribbon, a tiny braid of my own hair. I had been vague when Gryffin asked me what they were supposed to signify, though in my own mind I was very clear. They were feminine items. Things that might appeal to a young woman.

I wanted a chance to be seen as a girl. I wanted to wear clothes that were more flattering, cut my hair in a fashionable style. Sometimes when my mother was gone from the house, I tried on one of her dresses, though she was both shorter and heavier than I was and her clothes did not come close to fitting. But I wanted to know what they felt like. I watched the mirror as I spun around, and laughed to feel the swish of fabric around my legs. Once I sorted through her cosmetics and applied color to my cheeks and mouth. I looked strange and imperfect, but different.

I wanted to be different.

I did not express this to Gryffin.

We lit the little wreath and let it burn on the dry ground, then I ran around stamping on all the scraps of dead leaves that had started to smoke. The fear of accidentally burning down the tavern made us wait outside another thirty minutes, shivering in the dark, to make sure no fugitive sparks survived my fervor.

"I think it's safe to go in now," I said through chattering teeth. "It's too cold for fire to even burn on a night like this, anyway."

Gryffin laughed. "Good night, then."

"Warm Wintermoon wish to you," I said, and turned to go.

But he called after me. "Wait!" When I obediently

turned back, he maneuvered a few steps closer, till his canes were resting on the ground on either side of me. I realized to my surprise that Gryffin was actually taller than I was, and by a considerable margin. He had to bend down to kiss me on the cheek, something he had never done before. His mouth was almost as cold as my own skin.

"Warm Wintermoon to you, too, Kellen," he said, and smiled.

I smiled back. "Things will be different next year at Wintermoon," I whispered. "I can feel it."

"Different how?"

"Wait and see."

The new year started off promisingly enough. I was doing unexpectedly well in school, passing all my exams and keeping clear of all my tormentors. Gryffin's health did not continue to improve so rapidly, but he didn't lose any ground, either, so both of us were happy. The mayor got word that Thrush Hollow would become an official stop for a new stagecoach line, and the Parmers won the bidding to open a posting house. They set about constructing a couple of large buildings just across the road from their rambling house. There was a restaurant, with a few sleeping rooms above it for travelers not interested in seeking out a true inn. In back were greatly expanded stables to hold the many changes of horses that would be required to accommodate the thrice-daily run of the stage. The speculation among townspeople was that a stagecoach line would mean the roads to Thrush Hollow would be improved, which meant that private traffic would increase through the town as well. Which meant bounty for everyone who ran a service of any kind.

As soon as I learned that the Parmers were opening an eating establishment, I sought out Sarah Parmer and asked for a job.

She was no longer in school; she was working full-time for her parents, but everyone expected her to marry within a year or two. The man who loved her was Bo, the genial red-bearded driver who had first taken Gryffin and me to the Parmer house. He had been promoted from driver and was now tasked with overseeing the stables. Sarah and her mother would be in charge of the restaurant and the tiny inn; her father and brothers would continue running the freighting enterprise.

But there was a great deal of additional work to be done.

Sarah and her mother were painting the interior of the restaurant when I showed up. Everything looked new and smelled fresh. Tables and chairs were crowded into the middle of the room to make room for the workers; cheery red-and-white-checked curtains had been laid across a table, ready for hanging when the paint dried.

"I came to see if you'd hire me," I said, when Sarah set down her brush and stepped over to greet me. "You know I work hard. You know I can do almost anything."

"And there's a lot to do here," she agreed. "What were you thinking of?"

I shook my head. "I don't care. I'll cook in the kitchen. I'll work in the garden. I'll even help with the horses if some-one shows me how."

Betsy Parmer looked over at me from across the room. "Would you serve customers?" she asked. "You could cook when it was slow, and then serve when the stage arrived."

"That would be fun," I said with a little smile. "Get to meet all sorts of people that way."

Sarah surveyed me a little doubtfully. "Yes, but— Kellen—if you're going to be waiting on people . . . I'd want you to be in clothes that were a little less . . . ragged. I don't mean to tell you what to wear, but—"

I looked up at her, trying to keep the desperate hope from my expression. "Would I have to wear a dress?" I asked.

She bit her lip. "Well, I'm not saying that, exactly—"

"Because if I tell my mother I have to wear a dress or I can't get the job, she'd let me wear the dress."

Betsy Parmer put her own paintbrush aside and came to stand with us. She laid a hand on my shoulder and gave me the sweetest smile. I knew that I was about to benefit from another one of those rare, magical moments of kindness. "Sarah and I were saying just this morning," she said quietly, "how we would like to maintain a certain style here in the dining room. We thought maybe red aprons on the girls serving food, and red vests on the young men. This would go well with the curtains, don't you think? And we'll have red flowers on each table. If you're to come work here—and I sincerely hope you do—you'll have to wear some nice little gown, maybe in gray or black, that looks well when paired with red. Otherwise, I'm afraid we can't hire you. And we very much want to hire you, Kellen."

"Thank you," I whispered. "I'll tell my mother."

"How quickly can you start?" Betsy Parmer asked. "The first stage won't come through till next week, but if you could help out this week, we could put you to work doing all sorts of things."

"I can start now," I said.

Betsy nodded. "Then roll up your sleeves."

At first I thought I had guessed wrong about my mother.

"A dress," she said, when I told her the requirement for me to work at the new Parmer Arms. "But you can't wear a dress. That would look silly. That would be indecent. Boys wear trousers."

I sat up straight enough so that my growing breasts made a definite shape against my tattered white shirt. "Girls wear skirts."

She looked at me as if she hadn't noticed my changing figure before, and her eyes slowly filled with tears. "You're not," she whispered. "You're not supposed to be."

"I don't know what I'm supposed to be," I said tiredly. "But this is what I am."

As it turned out, she neither granted permission for me to take the job nor told me outright that I could not. She merely ignored my request, ignored anything that had to do with my new identity. She did not help me cut and sew the three gowns I made for myself, following an extremely simple pattern. She did not ask about the work or comment on the money that I handed over at the end of every week. She pretended, as she had pretended my entire life, that I was someone else.

But I rather liked the new Kellen, who was, in many subtle ways, different from the old one. This Kellen was not quite so fierce, so independent, so wary. She smiled much more often—though that might have been to hide her shyness. She was not used to being stripped of disguises, unfamiliar with the casual appraisal a man might turn on a woman of any age or degree of attractiveness. She always felt like she was on display, vulnerable, pulled out of hiding, a breath or two away from being starkly naked.

But she rather liked it.

I worked at the Parmer Arms four days a week—three evenings after school and one full day when school was not in session. At first, I walked through town, from my house to Sarah's, wearing my old boy's clothes and carrying my dress over my arm; I changed once I arrived. Sarah quickly decided it would make more sense for her to store all of my "restaurant clothes" at the Arms and made herself responsible for keeping them clean and mended. She also added two somewhat fancier garments to my small wardrobe, obviously having a seamstress tailor them after the template of the ones I had made myself. These dresses—one a dark navy and one a charcoal gray—were my favorite two things I owned.

Sarah also spent some time teaching me how to style my hair, though both of us tended to wear braids and buns to keep our hair out of the way while we were working. Still, she showed me how to soften my face with a few loose curls, and she trimmed my long, completely neglected locks so they fell with more grace around my cheeks. At times I didn't recognize myself when I looked in the mirror. And I was glad to see a stranger peering back at me from the glass that hung over the front desk at the Parmer Arms.

Most of the people who passed through the restaurant did not recognize me, either. True, the majority were strangers merely stopping briefly for food or a change of horses, but the restaurant had become a popular place for townspeople who wanted to treat themselves to a special night out. The first two months I worked there, I waited on at least a dozen people whom I had known all my life, and not one of them knew who I was.

But there was one person who was not fooled by my new looks or my modulated personality, and that was Gryffin. Or perhaps I put that wrong. He did not seem to notice what I was wearing or how I had arranged my hair, if I was dressed like the most disreputable street urchin or a quietly stylish young lady. Whether I saw him at school, whether I dropped by his uncle's house, or whether I unexpectedly encountered him on the street, he always greeted me with a smile and my name. I did not bewilder or surprise him. He did not think I was trying to be something I was not, as my mother did; he did not think I was trying to break a chrysalis and become something I was meant to be, as Betsy and Sarah surely believed. He just thought I was Kellen.

I found this the most comforting thing that had ever happened to me. At times, when I lay awake at night, confused myself about what role I should take and what direction I should try to follow, all that kept me from slipping into tears was knowing that I was not completely lost if Gryffin knew how to find me.

Chapter Ten

t soon proved that one other person was able to identify me in whatever guise I assumed.

Summer again—the time everything always started. I had been working at the Arms almost every day for the past month, and greatly enjoying myself. I liked seeing all the strangers, trying to guess why they were making a journey and what kinds of people they were behind their frowning faces or harried words. I liked receiving Sarah's gentle praise and Betsy's easy affection. I liked being paid a handsome sum, too. I handed over much of my salary to my mother, but the rest I hoarded, determined to spend as little as possible on frivolous things. I couldn't have said what I was saving for, but I was certain that there would come a time when I would be glad to have a store set by.

On this particular day, I was approaching a table to wait on a dark-haired man and a rather old lady. From across the room, the man seemed to be Betsy's age, and the woman at least twenty years his senior—his mother, most likely. She had high, patrician cheekbones and silky white hair carefully coiled on top of her head. Her mouth was pursed as she studied her menu, and for a moment I thought she might be cruel, or at least unpleasant. But then she glanced up at me and I read her expression for what it was: pain. I had seen that often enough in Gryffin's eyes. I instantly felt sorry for her, and I gave her my best smile as I bobbed a curtsy to the two of them.

"Welcome to the Parmer Arms. Can I tell you anything about our menu?"

The woman opened her mouth, but did not get a chance to speak. "Kellen!" her companion exclaimed with every indication of delight. "I was hoping we would see you, but I thought we would have to come seek you out!"

It was the Safe-Keeper. I was so happy to see him that I nearly hugged him. "Ayler! I have been wishing you would come back to Thrush Hollow someday."

He laughed. "Why? Do you finally have a secret to confide?"

"Not at all. It is just that Gryffin and I liked you so much, and we have often wondered how your life was going."

"Very well," the Safe-Keeper said. "I am still taking my horse and cart all over the kingdom and learning the most outrageous things. How is Gryffin?"

"Oh, so much better than he was last year! There was a man here in the fall, studying to be a doctor, and he showed Gryffin how to treat his legs. Now he hardly ever has any pain—he still has to use his canes, of course, but he can walk much farther. He thought he might try to go to the

Summermoon Fair this year, but I'm not sure—it's *so* far, and what if he got tired? But he still talks about it."

"And your mother? Still renting out rooms?" He gestured around the big open dining room. "I'm hoping this very nice new establishment hasn't lured all her customers away."

I grinned. "No, in fact, we have a steady stream of business these days because so many more people are coming through town. I've been working here so much that sometimes my mother hires a girl who lives down the street to work at *our* house. So we're feeling quite prosperous."

"I'm glad to hear it."

"What brings you back to Thrush Hollow?" I asked.

"You told me to come," he said, smiling in his absentminded way. "And to bring the Dream-Maker with me when I did."

I almost fell to the floor in a faint. I was sure my eyes must have grown huge with astonishment, but I could not keep myself from staring at the woman with him. She met my eyes with a little smile in her own, but she didn't immediately speak. By all reports, Melinda was not a particularly warm woman, not one to take the sick baby in her arms while its mother begged her to heal it, not one to grieve with a young girl whose father lay dying. According to tradition, the Dream-Maker was someone whose own life was full of trouble and woe, who endured bitter sorrow herself—while at the same time, her mere existence enabled other people, strangers, to attain the most precious desires of their hearts. If she passed through a town, it was as if spring followed in her wake: Love bloomed, children thrived, money was miraculously discovered in the garden. But her own life was blighted, filled with ruination and rue.

The story went that Melinda's life had not been quite so wretched—oh, her early years had been very bad, so people said, but she had not suffered much since taking on the role of Dream-Maker thirty or more years ago. Yet I looked at her now and saw grief in her face and hurt in her heart, and I wondered what loss she had suffered to make her look so sad.

I did not know how to address her; I had no idea what to say. "I am so honored to meet you," was all I came up with as I dipped into the grandest curtsy I could manage. Which was not so grand, to tell the truth, for I had not had much practice. When I straightened again, Melinda was offering me a somewhat wintry smile.

"Your name is Kellen?" she said. "It is nice to meet you as well."

I just stared at her and found myself unable to respond. Ayler laughed. "Perhaps now is the time to tell Melinda all your hopes and dreams," he suggested.

"I can't think of any at the moment," I said.

"Anyway, it does no good for you to tell me," Melinda said with a touch of impatience. "I have no power over which wishes get answered and which do not. The magic chooses whom it will reward."

"I wish Gryffin could meet you," I said suddenly. "He has so many more dreams than I do, and they're so much better than mine."

Melinda gave me another slight smile. "Every dream has value," she said. "There is no scale to rate their relative merits."

"Go find Gryffin and bring him here," Ayler invited. "We do not plan to leave yet for an hour or two. We are taking our trip in easy stages."

By the drawn look of pain on Melinda's face, I assumed the short stages were for her benefit. "Where are you going? Why are you here?" I asked.

Melinda gave a little shrug. Her shoulders looked very thin under the expensive silk of her dress. She had been a lady-in-waiting to the queen before she became Dream-Maker, if I remembered correctly. Or at least a person of some prominence at court, back when the old king was still on the throne. "I thought to travel around the country while I still felt well enough to make the trip," she said. "Bring as many dreams to life as I could. I have been in Wodenderry too long. I thought it was time the other cities of the king-dom had a chance to fulfill their desires."

It occurred to me that she might be very sick, perhaps dying. In which case I had to wonder how much power she still had to make a dream come true. In which case, I needed to get Gryffin here as fast as I could. "Let me bring you your dinner," I said. "And then I'll go find Gryffin."

I told Betsy I was leaving, and then I fetched two meals from the kitchen. Once I deposited the plates on the table, Ayler rose and followed me to the door. He smiled to see me take off my red apron and carefully hang it on a hook in the front closet. "You're looking quite well," he told me in an approving voice. "The work suits you."

"Has Melinda fallen ill?" I asked directly. "Is she dying?"

Ayler pursed his lips and assumed a more serious expression than he usually wore. "Sick and sick at heart," he answered. "She has recently lost some loved ones and she has been feeling the weight of age for a few years now. I think she is tired. I think she no longer wants to be what she has been so long. I think she would like to resign her position and she does not know how."

"What happens then?" I asked. "Who becomes Dream-Maker?"

Ayler shrugged. "Who knows? The magic makes its own choices."

I looked at him very hard. "You know, don't you? You're just keeping it a secret."

He laughed. "That would be a very impressive secret, don't you think? But as it happens, no one has whispered it to me."

"How long will you stay?" I asked. "I don't know how quickly Gryffin will be able to walk here. He is much more mobile than he used to be, but—"

"Another hour, perhaps two," said Ayler. "Once people realize Melinda is here, there will be a crush of visitors through the doors. Everyone wants to touch her hand, or say a few words to her or—or—just be in the same room with her a few moments, loosing their own desires into the air. She will stay as long as she can, but we need to push on. We want to spend the night in Movington."

"Then I'll be back with Gryffin as soon as I can."

I left the Arms at a light run, going first to the school-house where I thought Gryffin had planned to spend the afternoon. But he was not there, and Mr. Shelby said he had not seen him all day.

I had meant to keep this news to myself, since I did not want everyone else sucking up any magic Melinda might have left to offer, but it turned out I was not a Safe-Keeper after all. "Go to the Parmer Arms," I advised my teacher. "The Dream-Maker is there as she passes through on a jour-ney elsewhere."

The staid Mr. Shelby slammed shut the book he had been reading. "The Dream-Maker!" he exclaimed, scram-bling to his feet and stretching out a thin arm to grab his jacket. "Yes—I'll be on my way right now!"

Gryffin was not in his second-story room at his uncle's tavern, though I found the door open once I had dashed up the stairs. He was not in the kitchen helping his aunt with the cooking, and Dora merely shook her head when I asked if she knew where I might find him. He was not in the front room, tapping kegs for his uncle, a task he sometimes per-formed when the tavern was very busy. He was not out back on the bench, though I checked again in case I had missed him on my way in.

He was not in any of the nearby buildings where I knew he sometimes took shelter from his uncle's moods—the bakery, the stables, the home of one of the children he tutored.

He was not, when I made the journey all the way across town just to make sure, at my mother's house, looking for me. "Why are you here?" my mother asked, startled, when I appeared in the doorway.

"Searching for Gryffin. I can't find him." He had only been to my house a few times, since it was a considerable walk from his uncle's place, but he had been so strong in recent months that he had made the journey more than once. My mother didn't particularly like him, for she considered him peculiar, but she was always polite to him.

"I'm sure he'll turn up sometime," she said without much interest.

"No, I have to find him now, before Melinda leaves."

Her sharp face sharpened. "Melinda? The Dream-Maker? Is *here*?"

See, I had gone and told the secret again. "Yes, at the Parmer Arms. With Ayler. But she'll only stay an hour or so."

My mother checked the dish she had cooking in the oven. "You stay and watch dinner," she said. "I'm going to go introduce myself to the Dream-Maker."

She was never so astonished in her life when I refused. "No. I have to find Gryffin. Just take the pan out and let dinner spoil for once. Go see Melinda, but I've got to keep looking."

And before she could think of how to answer me, I was out the door and running down the street. I was sure she would stand there a moment, wracked by uncertainty— waste all the ingredients of a good meal, or hurry up to the north edge of town to lay her dreams before Melinda?—but I was equally sure she would make the decision to go. I knew what she would be begging for, too.

To see my father again. She mentioned him so rarely that it was possible to believe she had forgotten him, but I knew she hadn't. Every time a packet arrived from him, she checked it first for a letter, which was never there, and then for the money, which was never much. But she never forgot him. She never stopped hoping.

I was certain that we had seen the last of him, that—until the day I died—I would never lay eyes on my father again. So I felt a wrenching sadness for my mother, who would take a dream so hopeless and present it to the one person she thought might make it come true. And I wondered how many other desperate dreams might be flung at Melinda's feet, how many other impossible desires people carried around in their hearts, despairing of a chance to ever speak them aloud. How many other people would crowd through the doors at the Parmer Arms, laden with unattainable wants, how many would be crushed by disappointment as the weeks passed and nothing in their lives materially altered? Was it better or worse to have the chance to say those dreams aloud, and then be forced to acknowledge that they would never come true? Was it better to live without dreams at all?

Surely not. Surely having the dream in the first place was what mattered most. The desire to do better, achieve more, consider the contours and colors of happiness. Surely that was better than to turn away entirely from hope.

I searched for Gryffin for an hour. For two. I searched for Gryffin long after I knew Ayler had loaded Melinda back into his little cart and turned the horse's head toward the eastern road. I returned to the schoolhouse, I returned to the tavern, I circled the entire town. He was nowhere.

Dark came early, swept in by a summer storm. I was back at my house, for I absolutely had to help my mother serve the dinner (a cold one of leftovers), clean up after the guests (a family of three, including a very cranky baby), and sort the linens for the morning (laundry day). Besides, it was by now raining so hard that I would not have been able to see Gryffin unless he walked right up to me and tapped me on the shoulder. I could not help fretting about him, wondering where he might possibly have gone and hoping he had found shelter from the weather. It had occurred to me that his uncle might have taken him somewhere—for instance, to one of the nearby farms where Frederick bought produce—and that Gryffin's absence might be mysterious, but hardly sinister. And yet I felt such great uneasiness that it completely overshadowed the disappointment I had felt at not being able to introduce my friend to the woman I was sure could change his life.

It was late, and I had just made up my usual pallet on the kitchen floor, when I heard a sound at the back door. I did not immediately pay attention, because the thunder had been so loud just then that for a moment I thought it had merely caused the wood to rattle against the frame. But then the sound came again—a faint knocking from a point very near the floor, as if a raccoon or a badger had made a fist and attempted a rather ineffectual pounding on the wood.

When I opened the door, a sheet of rain sluiced in, and Gryffin crawled in right behind it.

I cried out and pulled him deeper into the kitchen, slamming the door behind him. He was soaked through and his skin was icy to the touch. And his legs . . . He was using his arms to propel himself forward, dragging his legs behind him. It was clear by the ripped and filthy condition of his clothes that he had used this method to travel some distance, from wherever he had been all the way to my mother's house. It was not that he had somehow mislaid his canes. His legs were completely useless, not just twisted in their normal fashion, but broken, jagged, bleeding.

"Gryffin," I whispered, my throat so constricted that I could barely speak. "What happened to you?"

He dragged himself all the way across the floor till he collapsed in front of the stove, lying so close to it that it was clear he was trying to absorb any of its remaining heat. Behind him was a trail of water and dirt and blood. "My uncle," he gasped. "I made him angry. He told me to leave." He paused a moment to catch his breath. "I told him I wouldn't. He—he went and got his cart. He threw me in the back. He took me to the edge of town, and farther. I don't know how far. Then he—then he—"

It was clear what his uncle had done then. Beaten a helpless boy and left him broken, miles from shelter. I was full of such fury that I thought my bones would literally explode from my body. I was full of such grief that I thought my heart would stop. I was full of such fear that it was as if my blood had turned to prickling brine. Gryffin was so cold and so hurt and so desperate that I thought he might not survive.

"Let me see, let me see, let me see," I murmured, bending over him and, with shaking hands, trying to gauge the extent of his injuries. I knew nothing about medicine and had never even learned to set a bone. There was no official doctor in Thrush Hollow, but there were two women who served as midwives, and I had seen Mr. Shelby fix a boy's shoulder once when it got dislocated at school. "Gryffin, I want you to lie here very still—don't move a muscle—and I will go find someone to help you."

"No one can help me," he said, and he was sobbing. "Oh, Kellen, I think I'm going to die!"

At that point, if Melinda had been standing right in front of me, I would have sacrificed every wish I had ever held in my heart. I would have given up any hope of my father's return, my mother's love, my life eventually running some kind of normal course. I would have said to her instead, "Please save him. There is nothing else I want."

I heard a sound at the door leading to the interior hallway, and I looked up. Standing there was the father of the irritable infant, the man who was sharing the guest room with his wife and child. He was staring down at us, his face stupid with sleep, his hair rumpled from contact with his pillow.

"The baby's crying," he said in a dazed voice. "I came to get some milk. But—but—what's wrong with *him*?"

I came to my feet, feeling dizzy. "He got hurt," I said

brusquely. "Broke his legs. There's milk in the ice chest in the pantry."

But the man dropped to his knees beside Gryffin and very gently touched the worst of the open wounds, where the edge of a bone protruded. "I work with horses at my father's farm," he said. "I can set a bone. These are bad, but if you help me, I can help him."

So perhaps Melinda had granted my wish after all.

Chapter Eleven

We labored over Gryffin for an hour, the young groom and I. His name was Del, and he seemed to have forgotten all about his temperamental baby. He had me fetch a bottle of whiskey—something we kept in the house so rarely it was another miracle that one was on hand—to pour over the bleeding skin to combat infection. He had me boil water, mix a poultice to his instructions, tear up clean linens, prepare two sets of splints. I cannot imagine how Gryffin bore the pain of our ministrations without howling aloud, but he remained conscious and generally silent as Del and I set and bandaged his bones. His face was gray, though, as we finally laid him back on the pallet, and his mouth was red where he had bitten his lips to keep from crying out.

"This is bad," Del said when we were finally done and washing our hands. "I can see his legs were in poor shape to begin with, but now—"

"Will he die?" I demanded. It was all I could think about.

"Shouldn't," Del said. "Unless fever comes, and it might, what with his exposure to the rain on top of everything else. Shouldn't die, but, Kellen, I don't know that he'll ever walk again."

"I don't care about that," I said, though Gryffin almost certainly did. "I just want him to live."

In the morning, my mother found me sleeping beside Gryffin on the kitchen floor. After her initial gasp of outrage turned to a muffled exclamation of horror, she was relatively helpful. She assisted me in moving Gryffin to the parlor (where the sofa was currently unoccupied by a paying guest) and getting him cleaned up. She even found some of my father's old clothes—much too big, of course—and helped Gryffin change into them so he could get out of the bloody tatters he had slept in the night before.

Del came straightaway to check on us and seemed to think Gryffin's legs looked good. "How do you feel?" he asked.

Gryffin's face was strained and white. He shook his head. "I hurt a lot."

Del nodded. "I imagine you do. I don't have anything to give you for the pain, but there might be someone in town who sells something like that."

I stood up. "I'll go see."

"First you'll help me get breakfast on the table," my mother said. "You can see to Gryffin later."

"I'd like some tea, if you're making any," Gryffin said. I think he could tell how furious I was at my mother's unsympathetic response, and this was his way of encouraging me to make the meal as she'd asked. I nodded tightly and returned to the kitchen. My mother went to set the dining-room table, and Del stayed to talk with Gryffin.

In a few minutes, my mother joined me. "How are you going to get him back to his uncle's?" she asked. "He can't walk. Will Frederick come for him?"

"He's not going back to Frederick's," I said. "Frederick beat him and left him on the road to die."

Her face showed shock and disbelief. "Nobody would do something like that," she said.

I looked at her a moment. "People do terrible things to other people all the time."

She shook her head. "Then I—what's going to become of him?"

"I don't know."

She looked alarmed. "He can't stay here."

"Why not?" I said, my voice tired. "You've always wanted a boy."

Now her face was such a mixture of emotions I couldn't sort them all out—anger, grief, guilt, confusion. I rushed on before she could think of something to say. "I'll find some-where else for him to go," I said. "But he'll have to stay here a little while. He can't walk. He can hardly move. You can't put him out on the street."

Her hands were shaking as she turned to the stove, and the pans rattled in her grasp. "No," she said over her shoul-der. "I won't put him out. But he'll have to go. There's no place for him here."

It was three days before our lives settled back into anything like normal. Del and his family stayed one more night, Del expressing a desire to do what he could for Gryffin, and I was deeply grateful for his aid. One of the midwives, an older, imperturbable woman, also was most helpful. Not only did she supply a range of powdered herbs that succeeded in easing Gryffin's pain, but she proved to have a wide knowledge of infection and how to prevent it, and she dropped by several times to check on Gryffin's progress. Mr. Shelby came to the house once with an armload of books and a great deal of sympathy, and stayed for dinner.

To Ian Shelby I told the entire story, but I could tell that he, like my mother, did not entirely believe me. Frederick was not particularly well liked, but he was well known; he was a long-standing member of the community. No one could believe that he would commit an act so atrocious— could believe it, would believe it.

"Well, now, surely there's been a misunderstanding," Mr. Shelby said. "Surely there's more to the story than we know."

But I knew there was no misunderstanding. I knew that Frederick had tried to murder his nephew.

And he knew I knew.

The evening of that first day, after the guests were fed and the dishes were done and Gryffin was reclining as comfortably as possible on the sofa, dosed with the midwife's drugs, I silently left the house. I trudged the mile to the tavern, entered the back door without a challenge, and rummaged through Gryffin's room to find such items of clothing as I thought he might be able to use. There wasn't much. I had brought a small bag with me to carry his clothes home, and I did not entirely fill it.

Then I headed back downstairs and stopped in the kitchen, to find Dora and some servant girl feverishly making meals.

"I need to talk to Frederick," I said.

Dora gave me one quick, harassed glance. "He's busy."

"I need to talk to him tonight. Tell him I'll wait out on the bench in back for a while. After that, I'll come look for him in the tavern." I paused. "I think he'd rather talk to me in private."

Now the look on Dora's face was pinched and worried. I could see her mouth open, her lips pursed as if she had a question to ask. *Where's Gryffin?* you'd think she might want to know. Or, *Have you seen Gryffin? Is he all right?* But she didn't ask either question. She didn't say anything. She merely nodded and went back to her cooking.

I went outside and sat on the stone bench, my bag between my feet. Last night's storm had cooled the air remarkably; the world felt clean and eager, full of possibilities. I was exhausted, though. I had been awake half the night and working hard since I'd woken up. I let my shoulders sag against the back wall of the house, and waited without impatience.

Twenty minutes after I sat down, Frederick came out of

the tavern. His face was drawn into a scowl, and he was drying his big hands on the front of his shirt. "What do you want?" he said in an unfriendly voice.

I came to my feet. "You didn't kill him, you know," I said quietly.

He stood very still and just looked at me.

"You tried to kill him, but he's alive. He's at my house."

Frederick grunted. "Maybe I'll have another go at him, then."

I stepped closer, which I could tell surprised him. He eyed me uncertainly. My voice was even softer when I spoke once more. "If you ever touch him again, I will call every Truth-Teller in the kingdom to this town," I said. "I will have them stand on every street corner and inform everyone that you tried to kill your nephew. They will describe how you beat him, because he was too weak to run away from you. They will tell everyone how you turned your tavern into a brothel, sending couples up to Gryffin's room for a little fun."

Now his face was red and angry. "I didn't do any of that!"

I raised my voice. "What else will Truth-Tellers repeat if they come here to talk of you, Frederick? Did you rob your customers? Did you beat your wife? How many times have you lied and cheated? The Truth-Tellers know everything—and they will tell everyone."

"You brat," he hissed and swung a hand to strike me.

I dodged the blow and punched him hard in the stomach. I heard his breath *whuff* out, and his face grew stupid

114

with surprise. No one ever expected me to be as strong as I was. He staggered back and put a hand up against the wall to steady himself.

"If you touch him," I said. "If you speak to him. If you *look* at him. Everyone will know what you have done."

"Call a Truth-Teller to do your bidding, and he'll talk about *you* as well," Frederick wheezed. "Everybody knows that."

I laughed. "Why would I mind if anybody talked about me? I'm a lost girl who dresses as a boy who nobody in the world cares about. I don't have anything to hide."

Frederick had pretty well recovered by now from my earlier blow. Now he straightened and took another menacing step toward me. Ayler had taught me where to kick a man to do the most damage, and I was strung with tension, ready to do just that, but he didn't come near enough to offer me an opportunity. "Everybody hides something sometime," he said. "You better be careful."

I wanted to kick him anyway, just to see him suffer, just because he was loathsome and cruel and deserved so much more pain than I could ever inflict. But I didn't. I stepped away. "You've already hurt me so much by hurting Gryffin," I said softly. "There is nothing more you can ever do to cause me pain."

On the evening of the third day, I told Gryffin about Melinda. He was feeling well enough to sit up, and his appetite was good, and the aching in his legs was not as severe. He still required a great deal of care, and my mother was still disgruntled that he was taking up what might otherwise have been a paying bed, but he was improving, and that was good enough for me. He had slept much of the day and was wide awake now at what was close to midnight. Everyone else in the house—my mother and an elderly couple who had rented the room for four nights—was asleep. I had just crept in from the kitchen to do one final check on Gryffin and found him propped up and staring moodily at one of Mr. Shelby's books. He wasn't even pretending to read, just sitting there with the volume open on his lap.

"Are you in pain?" I asked with some concern.

He looked over at me and attempted a smile. "No. Well, not much, anyway. I just find that my mind can't settle."

I came to sit beside him on the sofa, as I had every couple of hours for the past few days. I checked his forehead for fever, but his skin was cool. I checked his bandages for fresh blood, but they were clean. The mug beside his bed was still full of water. There didn't seem to be much I could do for him except distract him.

"I was looking for you, you know," I said, leaning back against the cushions. Gryffin relaxed beside me, and our shoulders touched. I could feel his thin hipbone resting against my own. "That day when you went missing."

"That's what you said," he replied. "But you never said why."

I gave a little laugh. "That's right, I didn't! How is that possible? Because I had very exciting news. I suppose I've been too busy to remember."

"So tell me now."

"Melinda was in town. The Dream-Maker. Ayler brought her."

I felt Gryffin stir beside me. "She *was*? Did you talk to her? What was she like?"

"She looked old and sad, I thought. Ayler said she was in mourning. And she looked—I wouldn't have said I thought she seemed like a *kind* person, but she looked interesting. As if, if you asked her about her life, she would have no end of fascinating stories to tell."

"Did you ask her to make any of your dreams come true?"

I shook my head, so the ends of my hair brushed against the top of Gryffin's shoulder. "I wanted *you* to meet her. I wanted her to grant *your* wishes. I should have asked her on your behalf before I ever left the Parmer Arms."

He let out a small sigh that might have been a laugh. "Maybe you would have asked for the wrong things."

I shook my head more vigorously. "No, I wouldn't! I would have asked her to make your legs whole again. And then I would have asked her to make sure you got accepted by a school in Wodenderry."

He turned his head just enough to look at me, and he was smiling. "Maybe those aren't the things I would have asked for."

I was too tired to sit up in astonishment, but my eyes widened. "*Really?* Then what would you have wanted her to give you?"

Now he was laughing, but he shook his head. "Maybe I have to think up some better dreams before I present them to the Dream-Maker. What would *you* have asked for? That's what I want to know."

I sighed and snuggled deeper into the sofa. My head tilted sideways till it was leaning on Gryffin's shoulder. "So many things," I whispered. "I want my father to do something to prove he cared for me. I want my mother to be happy. I want someone in my family to love me for who I am," I said. "I want you to be well, or at least out of pain. I want Sarah to marry Bo and have a splendid life. I want Mr. Shelby to find every book he's ever wanted to read. I want . . . I want . . . I want everyone I ever met to have at least one wish come true, even if they don't deserve it. That's what I want."

Gryffin was laughing now, silently. I could feel his shoulders shaking. He picked up my hand and held it in front of him, turning it this way and that, as if it was a rare and beautiful stone he had just rescued from a riverbed. "Those are some very generous wishes," he said.

"Except your uncle," I amended. "I don't want him to ever be happy again."

"And Carlon," Gryffin added.

I sighed. "Even Carlon should have one wish come true. But not Frederick. And you should get twenty for each one that all the other people get."

"So have any wishes come true?" he asked. "Since Melinda's been here?"

"Maybe. I don't know. I've been too busy to notice."

"It would be interesting to find out."

I yawned and sat up, still yawning. Gryffin dropped

my hand. "One of mine did," I said. "You survived."

He watched me seriously. His face was so pale that his blue eyes seemed especially vivid. "I hope you get more than one wish," he said.

I stood up. "It was the most important one," I said. "I don't have to ask Melinda for anything else."

In the morning, I walked up to the Parmer Arms, where I was scheduled to work a full day. The restaurant served a steady stream of local and out-of-town customers for the first three hours of the day, and then we had a little break about an hour before noon. I drew Betsy and Sarah aside. My face was so serious that I could tell they were both alarmed.

"I don't know if either of you heard that Gryffin got hurt a few nights ago," I said.

Sarah nodded. "Yes, Ian Shelby mentioned it, but I didn't get all the details. Will he be all right? I was under the impression his injuries weren't severe."

"They were bad enough," I said quietly. "Though he'll mend. But he can't go back to his uncle's house."

I saw instant comprehension come to both of their faces—and, unlike Mr. Shelby, they didn't seem inclined to doubt me. But I had learned my lesson about telling the whole story, and I wanted more than sympathy from them just now.

"When he's well enough to move, Gryffin will need someplace to stay—and someplace to work," I said. "You know he's good with his hands. And he's very smart. I wondered if you had tasks you could turn over to him. He could count money or keep your books—for the Arms as well as the freighting company. He can write out correspondence or hand-letter signs. He can even work in the kitchen, if you sit him down someplace and bring over all the things you want him to chop and slice. And I'm sure there's more he could do if you asked him."

Betsy and Sarah were exchanging glances. I often wondered if it made Sarah happy, just gazing at her mother, knowing how much she resembled the older woman and able to see what she would look like twenty years down the road. I had to assume she was pleased to see she would appear so serene, so kind, the sort of person anyone would be grateful to become.

"There's the mud room right on the back of the house," Betsy said. "Not very big, but big enough for a bed and a chest of drawers. No steps to go up or down, just a straight shot right to the kitchen."

"Bo made a wagon for his nephew last month," Sarah said. "I bet he could make a chair for Gryffin, something with wheels instead of feet, that would let Gryffin move around the house."

"Your father was saying just yesterday that he'd gotten his receipts all in a jumble and he didn't have time to straighten them out."

"And I'm wondering if perhaps we might advertise a service? 'Fair copies made here'? There must be travelers coming through who might need a little help with their letters. A lawyer or two working on a will."

"The menus," Betsy said. "We could change them every week, if Gryffin could write them out."

"Dinner specials," Sarah said. "He could make signs and we could post them in the town square."

With every word they said, I felt the pain in my chest grow sharper. I felt my lungs labor harder, but bring in less air. There was no room. Hope and happiness had lodged over my heart, and they were crowding out everything else.

Betsy turned to me with a smile. "We'll get the room ready. Bring Gryffin here when *he's* ready. We have lots of work for him to do."

Part

Two

Chapter Twelve

The year that followed was the happiest of my life.

It was a few more weeks before Gryffin was installed at the Parmer Arms. During that period of time, maybe twenty guests came and went at my mother's house. Summermoon arrived and was merry and departed again. I turned fourteen. Gryffin healed, but not completely. His legs were in even worse shape than they had been before Chase Beerin came to town, and his daily, ordinary level of pain was higher than it had been in years. The massages I still performed once a week gave him some relief, but not as much as before. I knew, because he told me when I asked, that places on his legs always felt like they were on fire. Night and day. Though he laughed and worked and slept and was only rarely snappish because of the pain.

Mr. Shelby had made him a new set of canes, coming to my mother's house to measure him for the proper height. And Gryffin forced himself to use them every day, making a slow promenade from the parlor to the kitchen and back

again. But I could tell the exercise was agony. Still, I was
awed by his determination, by his refusal to simply endure.
With Gryffin, everything was about the effort. He did not
mind failure so much as he minded the idea that he might
stop trying. It was hard to believe that anything would ever
make him give up.

Sarah's red-haired Bo showed up at my mother's house
one day with the contraption he had constructed—a heavily
padded chair that ended with four small wheels instead of
feet. Handles on the back allowed me to propel Gryffin from
behind, though he found that, inside my mother's house, he
could easily maneuver the chair by pushing himself off of
walls and furniture. He was so delighted with the chair that
he allowed me to take him outside in it and parade him up
and down the street in front of my house. The ride was
rocky, but he didn't mind, nor did he seem bothered by the
stares and whispers of the people we passed on our trial run.

"I don't think I've felt the sunshine on my face for five
weeks," he gloated, closing his eyes and tilting his head up.
He lifted his cupped hands, as if to check for rain. "It feels
easier to breathe, somehow."

"I'll have to take you out every day," I said. "Unless the
weather's bad."

"Even then," he said.

When he was well enough, I wheeled him all the way to
the Parmer Arms, a bag of his belongings strapped to the
back of the chair, another bag in his lap. Some passersby
still stared, but by now most of the people of Thrush Hollow
had had a chance to view Gryffin in his outlandish chair, so

they either waved if they were friendly, or ignored us if they were not.

Sarah and Betsy had set up a very small room right off the kitchen and filled it with everything Gryffin might need. The bed, the dresser, the basin of water—everything was at a height comfortable for a seated man to reach. Gryffin practiced moving his chair from the bedroom through the kitchen to the dining room, and found a few places too narrow for him to pass. Furniture was rearranged. The route was practiced again. Everything was flawless this time.

Gryffin was grinning broadly. "I'm all set," he said. "When do I start?"

It wasn't long before Gryffin became a fixture at the Parmer Arms. For the busiest of the working days, Sarah and Betsy had built a small desk for him at the front of the dining area, and here he had much to do. He answered questions for travelers when they first came in, for he had been equipped with maps, a list of stage schedules and fares, names of people looking for passengers to specific destinations, and other information. He handled all the money when people paid for their meals, and was scrupulous about counting coins at the end of the day. When the crowds thinned down, he organized the books for both businesses, and found several places where both Josh and Betsy could save significant amounts of money.

When there was nothing else to do, he read. He was still hoping to gain entrance to a professional school in Wodenderry, still studying in every free moment. Myself, I had pretty much given up the notion of further schooling, though Mr. Shelby dropped by the Arms every couple of weeks to try to cajole me into returning to the classroom.

"Between working here and helping out my mother, I don't have time," I told him. Though, truth to tell, I was doing very little work for my mother these days. I still helped prepare breakfast every morning, and I was on hand at least twice a week to do laundry, but most of the rest of my time was spent at the Arms. My mother could scarcely complain, since I gave her more than half of my salary. "Anyway, I already know as much as I need to, don't you think? I can read and I can count. What else is there?"

"I'm going to talk to Gryffin," Mr. Shelby muttered.

So Gryffin added to his list of chores the occasional hour spent tutoring me. I can't say I was a good student. I can't say I learned that much. But I wanted to please Gryffin, so I tried. I read more difficult books than would have come my way otherwise, and I enjoyed them. I studied more history. I practiced long division and improved my understanding of multiplication tables, but now and then I would still count on my fingers or ask Gryffin to solve it if the problem was too hard. But as long as I made the effort, he was satisfied. As long as I didn't give up.

Now that I was at the Parmer Arms every day, I began to be more familiar with the regular customers. These included the stagecoach drivers, a number of merchants of both high and low degree, members of wealthy families who were constantly traveling to Wodenderry on political business, and more ordinary folk who had family in other cities. I found I enjoyed getting to know them and hearing how their lives progressed—and, when they had good news, celebrating with them.

For that fall, there seemed to be an abundance of small victories. "Can you believe it? Jennie's pregnant! After all this time!" said one of my favorite customers, an ample and affectionate woman with an immense family scattered around the country. "She's growing so big I think there must be *two* in there! Well, she's just tickled."

"Did I meet Jennie?" I asked, for I had encountered so many of her relations that I could not keep them all straight.

"You did. She was with me—oh, three weeks back. Big girl, curly yellow hair. Horse laugh, which some people don't like, but it always makes me smile."

"Oh, I remember her! Well, tell her congratulations."

There was also the young man who had passed through with his family and stayed the night because his son came down with such a high fever that they were afraid to travel. He and his wife were still a little worried when they took to the road again the following day, and I had thought of them from time to time, wondering if the boy survived the journey. But when his father returned in a few weeks, he was smiling. Yes, the fever had abated. No, it had done no permanent damage. All was well.

In addition, all of us were closely following the story of a woman named Juliet who had come through on the common stage, traveling by herself and looking defiant but afraid. She was on her way to Merendon, where her uncle lived, to contest a will that seemed to give him control of property she had expected to inherit upon her parents' deaths. Gryffin had spent some time with her, as they puzzled over the terms of the will *she* believed was valid, and making a copy of it, which all of us witnessed. The copy remained behind at the Parmer Arms, while Juliet went on to the seaside city.

This was not, we soon learned, a matter that would be settled quickly. Juliet came through our doors about once every six weeks for the next few months, always with news of some new development in the case. A witness had been located, then mysteriously had disappeared. An investigator found even more money in her parents' estate than was previously realized—which was good, if Juliet won the case, but bad if her uncle did. A confused old servant changed her testimony so many times that it was impossible to believe anything she said. Juliet's lawyer grew impatient, informed her he had better-paying customers with more hopeful prospects, and quit the case.

"And now I must find another lawyer," she told us mournfully one afternoon as she sat in the Arms and ate an excellent soup that Betsy had prepared that morning. "But no one in Merendon will work for me. I don't know if my uncle has bribed them to keep away from this case, or if they just don't want the bother because they think it is not worth the money. And I've spent almost all of the money I *did* have—now all I can promise any lawyer is that I will pay him from the estate, if I ever prove it's mine. And no one will work for free, I'm afraid."

"So what will you do, then?" I asked. I was serving her hot tea and an extra biscuit, for which she would not be charged. Sarah had told me once that I could use my own discretion to give a needy customer a free meal now and then, and I knew she would not mind Juliet benefiting from this policy.

"I don't know," Juliet said, a note of hopelessness in her voice. She was a thin woman, perhaps thirty-five years old, with very dark hair worn always in a severe style. Her face was plain, but I thought she was pretty when she smiled. She didn't smile often. "I think I'll go home and work for a while, saving as much money as I can, and then I'll try again. Maybe by then there'll be some new young lawyer in Merendon who thinks my case is good and is willing to help me try to win it."

There was a muffled laugh from the table directly to Juliet's right. We both looked over in some indignation to see who was auditing our conversation and finding it amusing.

"Raymond," I said, my voice reproving. "You of all people should not be mocking others' misfortunes."

Raymond was a strange man who had lately been a frequent visitor to the Parmer Arms. He was, oh, sixty, with a full head of snowy white hair and a smile of great charm—when he was sober. It seemed clear that he had once been a man of some standing who had fallen upon hard times, for he was clearly both educated and genteel, though very, very shabby. I didn't know if alcohol had been his downfall or if he had turned to the bottle when his other prospects disappeared. Now he made a meager living running errands for wealthier men, carrying small packages between cities for people who were too busy to do the task themselves, and completing other odd jobs. Josh hired him from time to time to work in the stables, though he wouldn't allow Raymond to drive any of his horses. "Can't trust 'im," was the freighting man's simple assessment. "Might start out sober, but there's no way to be sure he'll stay that way. And my horses are worth far more to me than he is."

Raymond came somewhat unsteadily to his feet and gave us both a graceful bow. "My dear ladies," he said. "I mock, but I do not mock you. I mock what was once the most brilliant legal mind in the entire kingdom! I have sat in consultation with the queen. I have outargued foreign ambassadors and pretenders to the throne. I have solved legal tangles that sat for two centuries before the court, miring five families in bitter dispute. For two decades, if anyone in the land needed a lawyer's help, the first question would be, 'Can we secure Raymond? Will Raymond take our case?'"

Juliet and I looked at each other uncertainly. "Is that true?" Juliet asked me in a whisper. "Do you believe him?"

"I don't know," I replied.

"And why should you?" Raymond demanded. "Look at me! Fallen so far from grace I might as well have been born a beggar's son. Not the sort of man to inspire confidence, and well I know it."

"What happened to you?" I asked outright.

He made a broad gesture with his hand, signifying matters too great to summarize. "A mistake in judgment—an attempt to rectify—another error," he said. "Then a cycle of censure, regret, disdain, and remorse in a continuing spiral downward until all that was left was the pathetic and nearly useless man you see before you today. But I was great in my time. *That* you should believe."

"Well, I'm sorry for you," Juliet said, since it seemed he was expecting us to say something. "You are a lesson to us all."

"I don't want to be a lesson," Raymond said irritably. "I want to be a tool."

Juliet and I again exchanged baffled glances.

"I can help you," Raymond said, enunciating very clearly. "I can win this case for you. If you trust me."

Now Juliet and I were completely silent.

Raymond took a couple of wavering steps over to our table, pulled out a chair, and, uninvited, seated himself. "You have a will. Your uncle has another will. One of them is authentic, but which one? In my experience, it is the man with the greatest resources and the greediest heart who has the bigger incentive to lie. Besides, you're a nice woman and I like you. Therefore, I believe *yours* is the true document. I am willing to help you prove it in a court of law."

Juliet looked at him, half fearfully, half hopefully. "But how could you do that?"

Raymond smiled. "Ah. My expertise is most extensive. I know how to look at paper and determine its age—how to examine ink and decode when it was applied. You think I don't? There are ways, my girl, experiments that are very impressive when conducted before a credulous audience.

But I can do more than that. I know how to make people confide in me. I know how to convince individuals to tell the truth. I know the questions to ask, the possibilities to consider, the frailties that people will or will not expose when they believe their souls are about to be judged. And I can tell when people are lying under oath. Always. A very valuable skill for a lawyer to have."

"But—" Again, Juliet looked at me. "But why would you want to help me? You heard what I just told Kellen. I can't pay you, especially if I don't win."

Again, Raymond made an airy gesture, this one even more expansive. "It is not your paltry fee that would make your case valuable to me," he said. "I could not charge you enough to cover the time I would invest in proving your claim. No, no, what I want from you is your trust. What I want from you is the chance to win—one more time. One more case. To prove to myself that I am the man I remember I was."

Risky on all levels! So much for everyone to lose! I could tell that Juliet was moved by Raymond's story, enough so that she might be willing to grant him this opportunity on his own behalf, forgetting her own dire needs. I could tell that Raymond, despite his grand gestures and the exaggerated lightness of his voice, was so desperate for Juliet to accept his offer that he would almost be willing to perjure himself for a chance at redemption. So much to lose—so many places to go wrong.

Juliet appealed to me. "What should I do?"

We needed the input of someone much more clever

than I could claim to be. "Let's ask Gryffin," I said.

When I motioned to him, Gryffin left his station behind the front desk and wheeled over to join us at Juliet's table. I pulled up a chair and sat beside him. Sarah threw me a curious look but did not come to investigate. She just went to fetch one of the other workers from the kitchen to cover the cash box while Gryffin was involved in the consultation.

It did not take long for Gryffin to assimilate the facts. "What occurs to me first," he said, "is the possibility of calling in a Truth-Teller. Can't this matter be resolved in a few moments if one of them were to point to the proper document and say, 'This is the one that's valid'?"

Raymond snorted with laughter. "Yes, you've just put your finger on the weakness of the entire legal system," he said. "For any lawyer, and any judge, and any plaintiff will take the word of a Truth-Teller! But it seems to be that once a matter gets tangled up with the law, Truth-Tellers lose the ability—or the desire—to straighten out the knots. Many's the lawyer who advised a client to seek a Truth-Teller's word before dragging a matter into court, but once a case has been dirtied by the law, well, only the law can clean it up again."

"Then if that option is out, we must look at this another way," said Gryffin. "We need to consider how much damage can be done if Raymond takes the case and is not successful. Is that Juliet's last chance to prove the validity of her claim?"

"It might be," Juliet said. "I am low on funds, and I'm growing so tired. I cannot spend the rest of my life pursuing this matter. I must either secure my parents' property or go on with my life."

Gryffin nodded and looked at Raymond. "And you," he said gravely. "If you take this case and lose. What does it mean to you?"

"Everything, my dear boy," Raymond said, still in that airy voice. "I will not again have the courage to approach someone and offer my services. I will continue on as you see me, except even less so. I shall shrivel and shrink and eventually disappear."

Too much! Too much weight for either of them to bear if everything should go awry, as it so easily could. I could see both Juliet and Raymond realize that the stakes were too high. I could see the sparkle of hope flee from both their faces, turn them heavy and sad.

"What do you want to do?" Gryffin asked Juliet in a quiet voice. "Everything points to the likelihood that this is a terrible idea. But does your heart agree, or does your heart rebel?"

"I want to trust him," she whispered. "I want him to try."

Raymond straightened in his chair. Gryffin nodded.

"Then I think you should let him," Gryffin said. "Give him the case."

Chapter Thirteen

We knew, because Raymond warned us, that we might have some weeks to go before we learned the outcome of Juliet's suit. But it was one of the topics all of us talked about—Gryffin, Betsy, Sarah, and me, as well as a few of our more familiar customers—whenever we had an idle moment. Whenever Raymond or Juliet passed through Thrush Hollow on the way to or from Merendon, we asked a dozen questions. I was so hopeful, and so afraid. And it was strange to me that I could care so much about the fates of virtual strangers.

But life went on unheeding as we awaited the verdict. The weather turned bitter as Wintermoon approached. I discovered, to my delight, that the Parmers planned to build a big bonfire behind the restaurant, and that Gryffin and I were welcome to join them as they burned the wreath. And what a wreath it was. For three weeks before the holiday, Sarah had set out a basket by Gryffin's desk and invited customers to contribute any small items they'd like to see burned at the bonfire. I had not thought the basket would fill up very fast, but I was wrong. Apparently there were all sorts of folks who didn't have the time or the place or the energy to weave their own greenery, but they liked the idea that their wishes could be tied to some big communal wreath and sent on their way with a burst of flame. Into the basket went ribbons and buttons and buckles and candle bits and quill pens and goose feathers and mismatched shoes and baby's clothes and lace caps and smooth stones from the river and so many other items I almost could not count them all.

I was also surprised to find that a number of guests scrawled their wishes on scraps of paper, rolled them into scrolls, tied them with ribbon, and dropped them in the basket. Juliet had even come through one day, leaving a piece of paper on which she had boldly written LAST WILL AND TESTAMENT. You could hardly get less subtle than that, I thought.

"So you mean, you can just write down what you want and *ask* for it?" I demanded from Sarah. I had always thought the wish had to be bounded by metaphor.

Sarah laughed. "I have seen many people do so," she replied. "I don't know if the direct request is more likely to be answered."

Josh and his sons took a day to weave the wreath. Gryffin and I spent the next day attaching all the customers' contributions to its springy green branches. Now and then we would stop and hold something up—a carved wooden horse, a child's broken flute—and wonder aloud what sort of wish it was supposed to represent. Sarah came by late in the day and wrapped a length of white tulle around the bottom curve of the wreath, tying it in a huge white bow.

"There," she said, with a somewhat embarrassed smile. "That's for a wedding."

Betsy attached dried fruit for prosperity, and Josh added a handful of fake gold coins—minted for just this purpose—to represent enhanced income. Earlier in the week, Gryffin had taken a piece of paper, and folded it over and over so that it looked like a miniature book, and printed very small letters on the front of it: ACADEMY OF LAW. This he tied to the uppermost branch.

I had thought long and hard about my own wishes. Truthfully, at the moment, there was not much I felt I desired. My best friend was alive and safe. My own life was full of purpose and excitement. I was continuing to dress like a young lady, growing more at ease in my feminine identity, though at times it still felt assumed. I was well, I was happy. I had no worries. So what I asked for was more of the same. I had found a broken pocket watch left under one of the restaurant tables one day. No one had been able to repair it, not Gryffin or Josh or Bo. So I took this and wrapped the cheap metal chain around the branches of the wreath, letting the watch itself dangle down like a fob.

"What's that for?" Gryffin asked me.

"Time," I said. "More days like the ones I have now."

We burned the wreath at midnight, seventeen of us gathered around the blaze. In addition to the Parmers, Gryffin, and me, there were a few stable hands who had nowhere else to go, and a handful of guests who were staying overnight in the rooms above the dining hall. Despite the cold, there was no snow on the ground, and Gryffin's chair was easily pushed through the dead leaves and fallen branches that littered the yard behind the restaurant. I had thrown a blanket over his legs so he had insisted I put on my boots. The two of us, therefore, were reasonably warm, but everyone else shivered despite the immense heat generated by the spectacular blaze.

"That's a powerfully fine bonfire," one of the guests observed.

"Needs to be," said Josh Parmer, as he and one of his sons rolled the giant wreath closer. "It's carrying a lot of wishes to the moon."

And after a moment to collect their strength and coordinate their efforts, he and his son hoisted the greenery shoulder-high and tossed it into the fire. Sparks shot upward and spit outward, and all seventeen of us loosed exclamations of awe and delight. I could smell the spicy scents of the burning spruce and Betsy's dried fruit; I thought I could see Sarah's tulle run with a filigree of fire. There went the ribbons, the buttons, the parchments, the dolls, Juliet's will, Gryffin's book. Turned to smoke and ash. A breath of desire exhaled beneath the perfect moon.

The new year was cold, snowy, and full of incident. Sarah and her redheaded suitor got engaged. Josh bought another two wagons and expanded his freighting routes. There was a fire in town, and three houses burned down, but no lives were lost. A young woman who had worked at the Arms part-time told us that she was pregnant and would be quitting at the end of the week.

She made this announcement in the middle of the afternoon after we had been just about as busy as we could stand. A few guests were still lingering in the dining room, finishing their hot tea and pie. The kitchen was a welter of dirty dishes we hadn't had time to wash up yet to prepare for the late stage and the evening dinner rush. Sarah stared at the young woman in some bemusement.

"But—you can't quit," Sarah said. "We need you. I was just about to ask if you'd like to expand your hours."

The girl took off her red apron and laid it over the back of a chair. "No. I'm too tired. All I want to do is sleep. My husband wants me home—he says things go to rack and ruin when I'm gone all day. I'm sorry, Sarah. I hope you find someone else to take my place."

And, just like that, she was gone.

Sarah and I were left gazing at each other. "Well," Sarah said with a sigh, "I guess we'll have Gryffin make up a sign and see if we can find someone who's willing to work. Last time, you remember, only three people were interested." There was so much commerce in Thrush Hollow these days that young men and women were too busy helping out their own folks in their small enterprises.

A teacup rattled in a saucer and a young woman sitting by herself stood up. "I'll take a job, if you're offering it," she said.

Sarah and I turned to stare at her. I had not been the one to wait on her, but I had noticed her when she came in.

She was perhaps in her early twenties and she was dressed like an upper servant, in well-made but unpretentious clothes. Her demeanor was also that of a servant in a wealthy household, for her expression was demure and her voice well modulated. But she was more beautiful than any servant I had ever seen, with luxuriant blonde hair piled up in a bun, creamy white skin, and dark hazel eyes with impossibly long lashes.

"You'd want to work as a serving maid at the Arms?" Sarah said finally, as if aware our long silence was rude.

The young woman nodded. "I'll wait on customers. I'll make up beds. I'll work in the kitchen, though I haven't done that as much."

"You have experience? You have references?" Sarah asked.

The woman's mouth twisted a little, but even that didn't make her less beautiful. "I've been working since I was twelve. I can give you some references from a few years back, but—but not from my most recent employer."

Sarah watched her steadily. "Why were you let go?"

"Not for stealing," the woman said quickly. "Not for doing anything dishonest." If we believed her, that still left an interesting range of possible reasons, from carelessness with the crockery to bad behavior with the butler. "I work hard," she added. "I'm honest. And I need a job. I swear, you won't be sorry if you hire me."

"Do you need a place to stay, too?" Sarah asked quietly.

The girl's shoulders sagged with relief. Not till then had I realized just how tense she was. "Yes," she said. "I don't know anyone in—" She looked around the room. "I don't even know where I am. I just got off the stage and stayed because I was too tired to get back on."

"Thrush Hollow," said Sarah.

"Thrush Hollow," the girl repeated. "You wouldn't think anyone would be able to find me here."

Her name was Emily, and everyone adored her within a week. True to her word, she was a hard worker who was not too squeamish to take on any task. She would even clear the mousetraps, something we had always made Sarah's brothers do, and never grimaced at emptying the chamber pots, either. Customers loved her and soon began to ask for her by name. Sarah's oldest brother began to hang around the dining hall more often, ostensibly to consult with his sister, but more often to flirt with Emily.

She and Gryffin were immediately fast friends, and she spent any free time she had during the day leaning up against his desk, talking to him. He reminded her of her little brother, she said, who had been born lame and died young. "I used to wonder what would have become of him if he'd lived," she told Gryffin one day. "And now I look at you and I think he would have done very well."

In fact, Emily spent so much time with Gryffin that I found myself not liking her quite as much as I should have. So what if she was beautiful and hardworking and kind? She must have some dreadful fault, or some dreadful secret, if she had been turned out without a reference. This fault was hard to see when she whispered something to Gryffin that made him laugh out loud, transforming his serious face. Or when she coaxed him to go walking with her outside on sunny days, exercising his battered legs as he rarely liked to do in cold weather. Or when she spent some of her first month's paycheck to buy him a book brought in by a wandering peddler.

"She thinks of him as her brother," Sarah murmured to me one day as I paused in the act of wiping down a table to frown over at Gryffin and Emily. "There's no need for you to be jealous."

Now I was frowning at Sarah. "I'm not *jealous*," I sputtered. "I'm—what? I don't care if they're friends. *Jealous*. That never occurred to me."

Sarah was smiling a little. "Oh. I'm sorry. Well, maybe you're frowning because you have a headache or something."

"I'm not frowning," I said, giving her a fierce smile.

"Good. Well. I'll get back to work," she said.

It was even harder to dislike Emily when she came across me one day standing before the mirror and looking hopelessly at my hair. Between working and planning for the wedding, Sarah had been too busy lately to help me much with my own appearance, and I was beginning to look almost as raggedy as the young man I used to pretend to be. I was startled when Emily moved into view behind me, and even more startled when she smiled.

"I can help you style it," she offered. "I used to be very good with hair. And cosmetics and accessories. I even know how to design a fashionable ball gown, though my stitches

are too big, I'm afraid, for me to make a respectable seamstress."

I laughed shortly. "I don't have much use for a ball
gown," I said. "But I surely would like to do something with
my hair."

"Tonight," she promised. "Come home with me and I'll
give you a cut."

She had taken a small room in the home of a widow who
needed the rent money; it was a place Sarah had found for
her when Emily first arrived. When my shift at the Arms
ended, I followed Emily back, and she built up a good fire in
the small grate. In it, she laid two sets of curling tongs, then
she lit a host of candles and set them around the room.

"I need good light," she said with a smile. "Usually I'm
not so wasteful."

She sat me in a chair in the middle of her room and
carefully separated my hair into distinct locks, combing
them this way and that, then snipping where she thought
appropriate. Next, the curling tongs, which sent a peculiar
burning scent into the air. Then she put a few pins in place,
holding the hair just so. "Now," she said. "Just a few touches
of rouge. And a bit of paint on your eyes."

"I don't want to look ridiculous," I said.

"You won't," she promised. "You'll like this." And she
worked on my face for twenty minutes, putting cream on
my skin and color on my cheeks. Finally she stepped back.
"All right," she said. "Now you can look."

I stood before her tiny mirror and stared. Such a pretty
girl stared back at me! Her grave face was framed by long

black ringlets, which were lightened with a pale blue ribbon. Her dark eyes were huge above slanted cheekbones, and her wide mouth, open with astonishment, looked plump enough to kiss.

"That's not *me*," I said, though the mirror image mimicked every word I said.

"You could go to the queen's ball, looking like that," Emily said. "If you had the right dress. If you knew how to dance."

I shook my head and my reflection did the same. "I don't."

"Well, you could do anything else you wanted to do," she said with a laugh. "Go on the stage as the lead in a play. Make someone fall in love with you."

I met her eyes in the mirror. "What did *you* do when you looked like this?"

Her smiling face was instantly sad and closed. "I didn't try such skills on myself," she said quietly. "I was the dresser for a wealthy girl. *She* was the one who looked lovely when I was done with my work."

"I find it hard to believe," I said, "that there was ever a place where someone didn't notice that you were the beautiful one."

She turned away and began packing up the items she had drawn from a well-worn leather bag. "Beauty is not worth the trouble it brings," she said. "You should be glad, Kellen. You can take on any coloring you want. I've watched you sometimes. You can almost disappear, if you feel like it. Sometimes, when there are rough men in the dining hall, you make yourself look as if you aren't even a girl. They turn away from you—they don't bother you. But you can be pretty when you want—all you have to do is smile, really, and people smile back because they like the way you look. You can present whatever face you feel like to the world. I've never been able to do that. People look at me, and they see my hair and they see my face, and they think I'm a certain kind of person. They don't see anything else."

I was sorry for her suddenly, and I never would have thought I could be sorry for this gorgeous creature. "That's not what we see," I said quietly. "Sarah and Betsy and Gryffin and me. We see someone who is kind, who tries hard, someone it is good to have as a friend."

"Yes," she said. "I was lucky when I landed here." She gave me a straight look from those deep hazel eyes. "I have not had much luck till now."

"I think Jack Parmer likes you," I said.

She laughed aloud at that. "So maybe I am even luckier than I thought."

After that, of course, I could not help but love Emily as much as everyone else did. She taught me how to curl my hair myself, and I bought a pair of my own tongs from a peddler who passed through. I liked the improvement in my appearance enough to use the tongs once or twice a week, but I did not like the investment in time, and I never grew interested in learning how to apply cosmetics. I was never going to be the frilly sort of girl that Emily was, or even a softly feminine sort of woman like Sarah. I was always going to carry around some of the toughness I had acquired in my years masquerading as a boy, and I would never lose the sense of independence I had acquired when I had been free to behave however I liked. So I was something of a hybrid— an original, as Sarah liked to call me—and I found myself content with that.

But then, for that year, I was content with so many things.

Chapter Fourteen

It was summer again—of course—when everything changed at once.

Juliet had arrived on the morning stage, on her way back from Merendon. Her face looked pale and drawn, and she had lost weight since we had seen her last. We all crowded up to her table as Emily served her breakfast, even Gryffin wheeling over from his post at the front desk.

"You look as if you've had bad news," Sarah said, pouring Juliet a cup of tea. "Maybe you should stay here for a day and relax. All the upstairs bedrooms are empty at the moment. We wouldn't even charge you."

Juliet gave her a brief smile. "You know—I think I might. I'm so tired. I don't think I can travel another inch today."

"So what happened?" I asked. I was always the blunt one. "Did you lose the case?"

She lifted the hot tea to her mouth and carefully sipped. "Not yet, but I'm going to. The judge drew me aside yesterday and told me I had best go home and sell any of my spare belongings. He was going to rule in favor of my uncle, and *I* was going to be charged fees for sustaining a frivolous lawsuit."

We all exclaimed in dismay at that. "What did Raymond say?" Gryffin asked.

"He wasn't there. I just left him a note as I was leaving. I felt so defeated. And poor Raymond—I know he's been trying, I know he's done his best but . . . I guess the case was too much for him. I don't know how he's going to react when the decision comes down. I want to be there to support him but I—I can't even support myself right now."

"Maybe you should stay more than a day," Sarah said.

Juliet tried to smile again. "Perhaps I should move to Thrush Hollow. Take a job at the Arms. I will have to be working somewhere, I expect."

"We'd be happy to have you," Sarah said. "We can always use more hands."

Emily pushed her blonde hair back from her face and smiled. "She can clear the mousetraps," she said. "Give me more time to chase off the possums."

"I hope you're not joking," Juliet said. "Because I might be serious. I have so little left now. Not even hope."

Just then the door blew back and a resplendent figure swaggered in. He was dressed in such fine clothes, and wore such a rakish hat, that for a moment I did not recognize him. Not until he had swept the hat from his head and bent double in a magnificent bow did I realize it was Raymond.

"Friends and acquaintances, best wishes on this most glorious day!" he cried. "Drinks for everyone! If it's too early to indulge in spirits, then refresh yourselves with tea! With lemonade! With any elixir you choose! We have cause to celebrate!"

Juliet rose to her feet, her face white, her hands gripping the edge of the table. The other dozen or so customers in the dining hall were all staring and starting to whisper. Raymond looked like a madman, but a happy one.

"Raymond," Juliet whispered, unable to find her voice. "Did you—what did—but the judge—"

"*Ha* for the judge!" Raymond said, sauntering deeper in the room, his fingers tucked into the edges of his suspenders. "The liar. The cheat! I knew as soon as I saw him he'd accepted bribes from your loathsome uncle. I've had dealings with the man before and knew he was not to be trusted. I just had to wait for him to make a move—to trip himself up, so to speak—and when I heard he had approached you yesterday—"

"I think I'm going to faint," Juliet said very clearly, and sank back bonelessly onto her chair. There was a flurry for a few moments as Sarah patted her cheeks and Emily bathed her face in cold water and everyone else in the whole restaurant stirred and muttered. Finally, Juliet was revived, though still pale. She stared at Raymond with eyes darkened by emotion. "Tell me," she demanded. "Quickly as you can."

With a flourish, Raymond pulled up a chair at her table and seated himself. "The judge was corrupt. But I have a few friends in Merendon from my more prosperous days, and I had them in place. One was a magistrate, who reviewed all the evidence as it was presented. Another was a very handy fellow who is good at sniffing out wrongdoing. He was there to overhear the judge send you off yesterday. Before the case had been settled! *You* did not realize that such an action signaled your willingness to forfeit your claim."

Juliet sat up. *"What?"*

"Yes! But only if you came to the decision of your own free will! For the legal code clearly states that any party may void his claim to restitution at any point, as long as he makes such voidance without duress and in good faith. But if he—"

"Raymond. Please," Juliet begged. "What is the outcome of the case?"

Raymond looked surprised. "Why, the judge has been remanded to the magistrate, of course. He confessed that your uncle bribed him to throw the suit in his favor. And bribery, as everyone knows, negates the rights of the party involved, which means your uncle has lost the case." There was a moment of dead silence as everyone tried to decide what this meant. Raymond added gently, "Which means that you won. The property is yours. I have the validated will in my briefcase."

Juliet shrieked, but the sound was lost in the general commotion of joy. Everyone was whooping, clapping, throwing their hands in the air. Emily hugged Raymond, Sarah hugged Juliet, I hugged Gryffin, and then we went round robin and hugged everyone else. Betsy came running in from the kitchen and screamed with excitement when she heard the news. No one in the entire dining hall could sit still to finish a meal. All the patrons were on their feet, and talking with one another, and telling their own stories of good fortune narrowly achieved. It was lucky that most people had already been served, because it was at least an hour before any of us thought to pay attention to any customer except Juliet.

"We must have a party," Sarah decided. "Tonight. We'll make a special meal, and we'll put up shaded candles throughout the whole room, and we'll turn away outsiders so it is just us celebrating with our friends. Gryffin, can you make decorations? Raymond, will you help hang them? Someone go out to the garden to pick flowers."

With a goal to work toward, we all became a little more focused, and the arrival of the noon stage clarified our minds even more. Juliet and Raymond sat at her table for nearly two hours, discussing the ramifications of her inheritance and what her next steps should be. I watched covertly as the hours passed, smiling to see Juliet's happiness, Raymond's decisiveness. They looked like different people from the ones I had first met. As if, like me, they had long had true identities hidden from the world, covered with careful masks. As if joy had allowed them to cast off those worn disguises.

The noon stage departed, and the day finally assumed its normal rhythms. Emily and I worked together to clean up the detritus left behind by the last wave of customers. We could now expect a few random visitors from this point until sundown, after which most traffic would be local.

"It almost makes you believe there is some good still in

the world," Emily said to me wistfully as we loaded up trays of dirty dishes.

"I believe it," I said, "but I can't always prove it."

The door opened, and a family of four crowded in. Through the front window I could see a fashionable carriage pulling up in the yard and the driver calling out for a change of horses.

"Back to work," I said with a sigh.

Emily handled the family while I served the solitary gentleman. He was handsome but morose, and hunched over his tea and biscuits as if nothing, not even food, could improve his outlook. "Can I get you anything else?" I asked him after it seemed he was done, though he had left half his cup untasted.

He looked up at me as if startled to learn another human being was in the world. "No. Thank you. No. I'll be going as soon as my carriage is ready."

Across the room, I heard one of our younger guests tell a joke and Emily laugh in response. She liked children, and I was always glad to give her the responsibility of waiting on their tables.

"That's very funny," she said in a cheerful voice. "Did it make your sister laugh?"

The man at my table sprang to his feet as if there were coils under his shoes. *"Emily?"* he breathed. And then, louder, almost crazily, "Emily? Is it you? *Is it really you?*"

For the second time that day, everyone in the room came to a frozen halt. I turned my head just enough to see Emily standing by the other table, a teapot suspended in mid-pour. Her face was as white as Juliet's had been; she looked just as likely to faint. "Randal?" she whispered.

And then the young man—Randal, I presumed—dashed across the room, actually leaping over a misplaced chair to go bounding to her side. He took her in his arms so forcefully that she dropped the metal pot and tea went splashing everywhere. "I cannot believe I have found you!" he cried. "Oh, my darling, I have looked everywhere for you! Oh, Emily, Emily, why did you run away?"

Whatever Emily might have wanted to reply to this was lost under his mouth as he kissed her with commendable fervor. Gryffin, Sarah, Betsy, Juliet, Raymond, and I exchanged glances of astonishment and glee, all of us slowly creeping forward from various stations around the room to get an even better look at this most emotional reunion. It was now fairly obvious what had been the cause of Emily's recent dismissal. She had fallen in love with the son of some noble family, and he had most definitely lost his heart to her.

Suddenly, with a sob of despair, Emily wrenched herself free and pushed Randal away from her. "I cannot!" she cried. "Don't you see—nothing has changed! Your mother sent me away, and she was right to do so. I cannot be with you, and I cannot endure to see you again! Go away, go away now, and never seek me out again."

Now the glances the rest of us exchanged were full of distress and dismay. But Randal, it proved, was not a man to be easily set aside. He came a step closer and caught her shoulders in his hands.

"Oh, no, I'm not leaving you ever again," he said. "Now that I've found you, I shall not let you go."

She was weeping. "I have told you once, I will not be your lover."

"I never wanted you as a lover. I want you as my wife."

Everyone in the room gasped. Clearly, this was a scene that should have been played out in private, but not one of us made a move for the door. In fact, I pulled up a chair, and Gryffin rolled up right beside me. Really, this was better than a Summermoon theatrical.

Emily cried even harder. "I can't marry you! Your family—"

"My family can rot in Wodenderry," Randal said cheerfully. "You and I shall live here—wherever here is—" He glanced around as if looking for a sign boasting the town's name. "Thrush Hollow" came from half a dozen helpful voices. "Here in Thrush Hollow," he concluded.

She almost laughed and tried ineffectually to pull away. "Oh, certainly. I shall continue to work as a serving maid, and you shall—you shall what? Open shop as a tailor? You cannot give up your inheritance, your *life*, for me."

"I have a small inheritance that will come to me no matter what I do with my life," Randal said. "And I am not above taking honest work. What is this place? A posting house? Perhaps they would hire me here." He looked around again. "Who's the owner, hey? Would you take me on? I'm good with horses."

Sarah stepped forward. She managed to keep her face grave, but her eyes were dancing. "I'm the owner's daughter," she said. "We're always looking for drivers."

Emily looked at her hopelessly. "He's not serious."

"I think he is," Sarah replied.

"I most definitely am," Randal said. "So who performs marriages in this town? Can someone go fetch him? I want to marry this woman. Right now. This minute."

Well, naturally that started an uproar such as none of us had heard since, oh, mid-morning when Raymond had arrived with Juliet's news. It was enough to make a person giddy, but it was a delightful dizziness, of anticipation bubbling just under the skin. Emily cried out that Randal couldn't mean it, and he countered that he absolutely did. Betsy sent one of her sons to fetch the town clerk, who performed weddings and recorded deeds, and the rest of us began conferring.

"Juliet, do you mind if Emily shares your party?" Sarah asked, and Juliet laughed out loud.

"I would be honored if she did," Juliet replied.

And so we made quick plans to decorate the dining hall with irises and summer roses, and to throw white cloths over all the tables, and borrow as many candelabra as we could scare up from friends and neighbors in the next two hours. Betsy was already in the kitchen, throwing together a wedding feast, and I ran upstairs to make sure the largest of the bedrooms was transformed into a bridal bower. Gryffin hand-lettered a sign that said PRIVATE EVENT—NO DINNER SERVED TONIGHT, and this was hung out front. Josh Parmer and his sons washed off the horse smell and changed into good shirts, then the youngest boy and Sarah's Bo tuned up their flute and fiddle.

And just as the sun was saying farewell with an ecstatic carnelian kiss, the serving girl and the young nobleman were married in the dining hall of the Parmer Arms. The room was tinted with sunset, candlelight, roses, and love. Gryffin and I served as attendants and signed our names as witnesses, and then Josh poured everyone a glass of wine. Raymond offered a complex and graceful toast that no one entirely understood, and we all lifted our glasses and cheered.

"Happiness to all," Juliet said, and we cheered that simple toast even more loudly, and we drank down the rest of our wine.

Into that scene of merriment, two men came strolling.

I was the first to spot them, and I went hurrying over. "I'm sorry, we're not having guests tonight," I began, and then I exclaimed in pleasure. "Ayler! It's been months since we've seen you! We're not letting strangers in, but naturally we shall make an exception for you."

Gryffin had turned at the sound of Ayler's name, and now he wheeled his chair over to greet the Safe-Keeper with a broad smile. "We have had such a run of good luck today none of us knows if he's standing or sitting," he said. "I find I'm actually glad I'm in my chair! Otherwise I know I'd fall over."

"Permit me to introduce my friend, and then tell me your stories, which I'm sure will be delightful," Ayler said with his usual abstracted smile. "This is Wendel. He's a Truth-Teller. We've been traveling together a good deal these past few months."

Gryffin and I politely introduced ourselves to the stranger, although, like most Truth-Tellers, he was not the sort of person you immediately found yourself liking. He was tall and thin, with an angular face and searching eyes. He did not look like someone who smiled often, even at others' random good fortune.

"So tell us," Ayler invited. "What are you celebrating? And can Wendel and I partake in the meal that smells so delicious?"

"It has been such an astonishing day!" Gryffin exclaimed. "Raymond just helped Juliet settle her claim against her uncle, so now she'll inherit her parents' estate and be very rich. And Randal just found Emily, who ran away months ago because his mother said she wasn't good enough for him to marry. But he found her anyway, and married her just a few minutes ago. We're toasting the bride and groom now. Then we'll eat. Then we'll have music, and maybe dancing."

"And of course you're welcome to join us," I put in. "We'll make up a table for you and your friend. Just don't be surprised if no one has any attention to spare for you tonight. We're all in a whirl, as you can see. . . ."

My voice trailed off. It was obvious that neither Ayler nor Wendel was listening to me. Ayler had been watching the celebrants, his usual sweet smile on his face, but Wendel was just staring at Gryffin. As if he had never seen a crippled boy before. As if he had never seen *any* human being before. As if the whole world had been made over in Gryffin's image.

The quality of his silence caught Ayler's attention, and the Safe-Keeper glanced from Wendel's face to Gryffin's. I saw his habitual smile deepen. "Ah," Ayler said, and then he looked at me. "More surprises," he said.

My throat had constricted; I put a hand to my face. "What?" I whispered.

But Wendel was ignoring all of us. He was still staring at Gryffin. "How can it be?" the Truth-Teller demanded in a harsh voice. "It's you."

Chapter Fifteen

ow the entire room fell silent, everyone else apprehending all at once, as sometimes happens in groups of people, that something momentous was occurring nearby. I felt the stares of all our friends, both a weight and a comfort. I heard soft footsteps and sensed people moving closer in one protective circle.

But I did not see them. I was staring at Wendel, who was still watching Gryffin. "What's me?" Gryffin said.

Ayler answered in his light, unalarming voice. "Last Wintermoon, the Dream-Maker pulled me aside and confided that the power had gone from her hands. She was both sad and pleased to be relieved of this heavy burden. But who had accepted the magic in her place? Who would be the one to endure great suffering while bringing great happiness to so many others?"

"Ayler kept the secret for two months, as she requested," Wendel said. His voice still grated against my ears. "But when no one stepped forward to claim the title, she sent him out to scour the kingdom, looking to see where the magic had found purchase. I was sent along to authenticate his discovery. But I never thought I would see the power vested in one such as you."

"Wait." That was Sarah's voice. "Wait. You're saying— Gryffin is the Dream-Maker? *Gryffin?*"

Wendel shook his head. "I've rarely heard of the magic going to a man before, and never to anyone so young. And yet it's true. You have the power of dreams and wishes in your hands."

Gryffin opened his mouth as if to speak, but it was clear he was too shocked and unsettled to know what to say. He wrenched his gaze away from Wendel and looked straight at me, confusion and uneasiness in his eyes. I knew that look. It was the expression Gryffin had always worn when he was lost or in pain. *Help me,* it meant. I stepped forward and took both his hands between my own.

"And no one I'd rather trust my dreams to than you," I said very quietly, and kissed him on the forehead. "All of us are safe with you."

Who knows how the rumor spread after that? Did one of Sarah's brothers slip from the Arms and go racing down the street to tell the girl he'd been courting that the power of the Dream-Maker had shifted into somebody else's hands? Did she repeat the news to her mother, who ran to her neighbor's house? Did that woman's husband head straight for the town center, and duck inside Frederick's tavern, and slam his hand on the wooden bar to get everyone's attention?

Something like that. For, not an hour after Ayler arrived

and Wendel made his pronouncement, the people of Thrush Hollow began arriving at the Parmer Arms. No one regarded the sign that asked for privacy. Everyone just stepped right in, knocking rose vases off the tables, helping themselves to meat from the wedding platters, crowding between the tables like sand pouring into a jar of stones. When no more could fit inside the dining hall, they began piling up in the yard outside, fifty, a hundred, two hundred. Within two hours, I believe, almost every soul of Thrush Hollow had gathered together to try to get a glimpse of the Dream-Maker.

"I never expected to have a wedding like this," Emily laughed as she helped Sarah and Betsy and me try to clear out the tables and make more room. "I think I'll be working through the night, not getting to know my husband."

Juliet was laboring right alongside the others, carrying dishes from the front hall to the kitchen, rolling up her sleeves, and preparing to wash. Betsy protested, but only once. After that, she accepted the assistance of anyone who was willing to help.

Raymond had taken charge of organization, setting Gryffin up at a table in the middle of the room and insisting all the visitors form an orderly line past him. Josh and his sons guarded the doors and made sure people entered at a reasonable rate and left after they had had their chance to speak to the Dream-Maker. Randal and Bo prowled through the yard outside—which now resembled a Summermoon Festival—to make sure everyone remained patient and no one caused any trouble.

It was dawn the next day before Gryffin had spoken to everyone who wanted to see him.

"Thank goodness that's over," Betsy said, as Gryffin slumped in his chair and the rest of us sprawled on whatever piece of furniture appealed to us, and she surveyed the muddy wreck of the front yard.

A soft laugh came from Ayler, who had done a brisk business of his own during the night, hearing secrets too delicate to confide even to the Dream-Maker. "Oh, no," he said. "It's just beginning."

And that proved to be true.

The months that followed were chaotic, exhausting, exhilarating, and full of magic. We doubled our business at the Parmer Arms—tripled it—there was no minute of the day that was not filled with patrons, asking for a room or a meal but really there to get a glimpse of Gryffin. Josh and his sons enlarged the restaurant and added a few more rooms on the second story to accommodate the influx of guests, and Randal took over the running of the auxiliary stables. People came from the entire kingdom to drop their hopes at the feet of the Dream-Maker, so we met people from all regions and all walks of life. They sat at adjoining tables in the restaurant and slept down the hall from each other in the rented rooms. Hearing their stories, learning their ways, was an education for me that would have made even Mr. Shelby proud.

We witnessed no end of miracles in those days, from lost children reunited with their parents to sick men rising up from their beds. But most often, the magic was more subtle and worked, if it worked at all, remotely and over time. Letters often came to the Arms months or weeks after visitors had been there, telling Gryffin how some impossible wish had come true. It was as if he was the epicenter of joy.

Yet Gryffin himself was not particularly joyous during this time. Indeed, in his determination to see everyone, hear every story, he was quickly wearing himself out. He lost weight; his face grew pinched and bony. He rarely complained, but when I asked him he would admit that the hours spent sitting in his chair, leaning forward to listen, made his legs and his back scream with pain. Between my increased duties and his, there was less and less time for me to draw him aside and rub salve into his legs—less and less time for him to practice his daily ritual of walking. I was afraid, and I knew he was, that if he stopped forcing himself to exercise, he would soon lose the ability to walk altogether. So now and then I would whisper to Sarah, and she would close up the restaurant a few hours early, and we would make sure that Gryffin had a little time to spend on himself. He was the Dream-Maker; he could not be allowed to waste away.

He was the Dream-Maker; his suffering would always be more than physical.

It had occurred to me to wonder, more than once, what his vicious uncle thought about Gryffin's new status. I had been tempted, so tempted, to send Wendel to Frederick's tavern the night that Gryffin's power had been discovered. I had wanted Wendel to stand in the middle of that crowded

taproom and shout aloud all the abuses that Frederick had
heaped on Gryffin and, probably, Dora. I had wanted
Frederick to feel the greatest possible remorse for how badly
he had treated the person who was, after the queen, the
most valued person in the whole country.

I didn't do it. But someone else did. And three weeks
later, the tavern failed to open. The man who delivered milk
to the kitchen found Dora stabbed to death on the kitchen
floor and Frederick hanging from the rafters.

Bo brought the news to me, and I waited till after dinner
to share it with Gryffin. It was one of the nights Sarah closed
the restaurant early. Emily made Gryffin practice his walking across the smooth floor of the dining hall, and then he
collapsed in utter weariness in his own small room. I went
in a few minutes later with a branch of candles in one hand
and a jar of salve in the other.

"Roll up your trousers to your knees," I instructed in a
businesslike voice. "You need to be worked on."

"I don't know, Kellen," Gryffin said, leaning back against
the pillows. He looked utterly spent. "I might be too tired for
a massage."

"Just a short one," I coaxed. "You always feel better
afterward."

"You must be tired, too," he said, cuffing and recuffing
the hems of his pants. "It doesn't seem fair that everything
in the entire world revolves around me."

I laughed and seated myself beside his bed. "The care
we lavish on you is an indication of the care we lavish on

our own dreams," I said. "You are the symbol. At least to most people. To me, and Sarah, and everyone else, you're Gryffin."

"And you cared about me before I had magic in my hands," he said. "That matters to me even more."

"I've been wondering," I said, opening the jar and stirring the contents with my finger. The cream had a light, floral scent and a thick consistency. "Did you know? Before Wendel arrived? Did you feel the power come to you?"

He shrugged against the pillows. "I felt—odd—for a few months. The skin on my palms burned now and then. But I often feel strange. I have pains I can't identify and bruises I can't explain. I didn't think anything of it."

I smoothed cream over his bruised, misshapen calves, and then I began to gently knead the muscles. "Even when everyone around you started having such good fortune? You didn't start to wonder, hmm, maybe what I'm feeling in my hands is a kind of magic?"

He laughed, the sound half a sigh. "No. Not really. Not everyone was having such good luck, anyway. Not all of you—the ones I care about the most."

"What can you possibly mean?" I demanded. "Everyone at the Arms has had a dream come true because of you. Emily and Randal are married, Josh and Betsy run the most lucrative business in town, Jack Parmer is engaged to that lovely girl down the street, Sarah will be getting married soon—"

"You're not happy," he said. "I've done nothing for you."

"I'm happy," I said. "I don't have any dreams right now, so there's nothing you could do for me even if you wanted to."

"You don't look happy," he said. "You look sad."

"I heard bad news today."

"Oh, Kellen. Did something happen to your mother?"

"No, she's doing well enough. Has had a full house for a solid week now and is feeling very prosperous. It was news that will upset you."

He was silent for a moment, thinking it through. "My uncle?"

I shifted in the chair so I could apply pressure to a different part of his legs. "Died by his own hand," I said. "Taking Dora with him."

He made no answer for a long time, so I did not speak. I merely continued working on his legs, pressing my palms against his skin, trying, with the strength in my hands, to push the bones back into alignment, untwist the knotted muscles. Finally he released a heavy sigh and settled deeper into the pillows. I looked over to see tears glimmering in his blue eyes.

"What sad lives," he said in a whisper. "Start to finish."

"I keep hoping," I said in a low voice, "that this is not my fault."

"Yours? How could it possibly be?"

"That one night. When Melinda was here. And I wished for everyone I knew to have a wish come true—except for your uncle. I wanted him to suffer. And maybe if I had wanted him to have happiness instead of pain, he would not have been so cruel. And he would not have died that way, and Dora would still be alive."

"That's not how the magic works," he said. "You can't wish it for somebody else."

"I think I can. I did for you."

"When? Oh, that night I almost died."

"So maybe you can give up your own wishes on someone else's behalf, or maybe you can give *some* of your wishes to someone else, but keep some for yourself, too. And I didn't do that. And now they're dead."

"And maybe he could have chosen to be a kinder person or Dora could have been a stronger person or maybe they could have made their own wishes," he replied. "Or maybe you can only make dreams come true for a rare few people outside yourself. The people you know the best. The people you care for the most."

I smiled and patted his legs gently, to indicate I was done. "Because seeing them happy is happiness for you," I said.

He lifted his hand up, fingers spread, and I laid my sticky palm against his. "That's why I want to see your dreams come true," he said in a low voice. "That's what I would ask for, if I had the power to grant my own wishes. To see you happy."

"But I am happy," I replied. "You have that power after all."

Chapter Sixteen

ut the truth was, I held a secret melancholy at the core of my heart. I did not voice it to Gryffin that night; I did not speak of it to Sarah or Betsy or Emily. I was happy now, but I knew there was sadness to come, at least for me.

And when, shortly after Summermoon, Ayler arrived at the Parmer Arms, I knew that sorrow arrived with him.

"Hello, Kellen, any secrets for me today?" he said, offering me his usual greeting.

"You know all my secrets," I said, pouring him tea. "Do you bring any news you can share aloud?"

He looked at me over the rim of his cup. "Not news so much as an invitation."

I nodded and looked away. "That's what I was afraid of."

He smiled. "I always thought you would have been a splendid Truth-Teller," he said. "There is never keeping any secrets from you."

"When will you take him?" I asked. "I assume the queen wants him in Wodenderry as soon as he is willing to travel."

"All the world comes to Wodenderry," Ayler said in an apologetic voice. "Thrush Hollow cannot make that claim."

I laughed shortly. "It can lately."

"By tradition, the Dream-Maker travels all over the kingdom, bringing the possibility of magic with her everywhere she goes," Ayler said. "But I imagine it would be too difficult for Gryffin to travel on a regular basis. So we need to set him up someplace where everyone can find him—even people who do not realize they are searching for their dreams."

"You can't make him go with you, can you?" I asked. "What kind of Dream-Maker would he be if you tied him up and threw him in the back of your cart?"

Ayler gave a soft laugh. "I wouldn't even try. But Gryffin has always wanted to go to Wodenderry, if I remember right. And Gryffin wants very much to do his best by his magic. I think he'll go willingly, if not with a high heart."

"Yes," I said, "I think he will."

Sarah and Betsy cried. Josh stood to one side, frowning, calculating how much the loss of the Dream-Maker would affect business. Gryffin looked terrified and excited and earnest, all at once. Ayler laid out his plan the day he arrived, went away for a week so we could all get used to the idea, and then came back one night in time for dinner.

"Ready to go in the morning?" he asked, and Gryffin nodded.

"Ready."

Gryffin and I had already said our good-byes—a dozen times, it seemed—but I went to his room again that night to

pronounce them one more time. He was in his chair, leaning over a suitcase that lay open on his bed, and his face still
wore that flurried mix of emotions that he had displayed
since Ayler first showed up.

"All ready?" I asked brightly. "Or do you need my help
fitting something else in your baggage?"

"I think I have it all," he said. He shut the case and pulled
his chair around to face me. "I don't want to go," he said.

I perched on the edge of the bed. "Yes, you do. You just
don't want to leave."

He laughed. "Maybe if you all came with me . . ."

"Not really possible, I'm afraid," I said.

He was silent for a moment. "Not for Sarah and Josh and
Betsy," he said. "But you could come to Wodenderry."

"I don't know anybody in Wodenderry," I said. "I would
be lost and afraid."

"You'd know me."

"Oh, Gryffin. You're going to be living at the royal
palace. You're going to be meeting with everyone from farmers to ambassadors. Your days will be so full you won't have
time to miss me."

"I think my days will be so full of missing you that I
won't have time for any of those other people," he said.

Now I was the one to stay silent for a moment. "It will
be strange," I said at last. "Since I was eleven years old I
have seen you almost every day of my life. I can't imagine
what it will be like to open my eyes every morning and
think, *Gryffin is gone*."

"And just as strange for me in Wodenderry."

"But you'll have Raymond, who lives in Wodenderry. Ayler is there much of the time. And you'll make new friends."

"Won't you come?" he asked in a wheedling voice. For the first time, I entertained the notion that he was serious.

"What does a fifteen-year-old girl do alone in the royal city?" I asked, for I had just celebrated my birthday. "Without a family, without a job? I can't think my prospects would be very good."

"You could ask Raymond," he said quickly. "He would help you find a job and a place to stay."

I considered. "I could. It's something I'll think about, Gryffin, I promise you. But for now I cannot leave. Too many people depend on me and I—I think you need to find your own place in Wodenderry. You need to learn how to live your new life before you start bringing bits of your old life into it."

He gave me a somber look out of those blue eyes. "You think I will forget you," he said, his voice accusing. "You think I will go to the palace, and make friends with highborn nobles, and drink tea with the queen, and forget about you. You think if you were there, I would start to find you embarrassing or annoying. You think that once I am the Dream-Maker in the royal city, I will be too good for you to know."

Now I was the one who was embarrassed, for that had been exactly what I was thinking. Not easy to lie to Gryffin, so I just shrugged. "I think a little of that may come true," I said. "I think you should see who you might become before you can be so sure you want to stay who you are."

He watched me a long moment, his face utterly serious, then he held his hand up, his fingers slightly cupped. I leaned forward until my cheek settled against his palm. I had spoken so calmly up till now that I had not realized how agitated I really was, how close to the brink of despair. But Gryffin's touch gave me back a measure of peace, transferred to my skin the knowledge of his own conviction.

"Whoever and wherever I am, I will always want you as my friend, Kellen Carmichael," he said softly. "If you won't follow me to Wodenderry, I'll have to come back to Thrush Hollow to find you."

I smiled widely enough that the corner of my mouth caught against the edge of his hand. "I won't put you to the trouble," I said. "I'll give you a year in Wodenderry. And if you still miss me, I'll come to the city then."

"What a great thing it is to be Dream-Maker," he said. "Just so will I be able to make my own dreams come true."

"If you have that kind of power, you'd better choose your dreams with care," I warned.

"My dreams have been the same since the days before I had any power," he retorted. "I imagine they will not change once the power leaves me."

"A year, then," I said. "I will see you then."

In the morning, Ayler came for him, and Bo loaded up the cart with Gryffin's meager things. We all stood out in the courtyard and madly waved good-bye. Then Ayler shook his reins, and his mare pulled forward in her traces, and the wagon moved forward, and then Gryffin was gone.

Chapter Seventeen

hat year was the longest of my life.

I think we all felt a sort of heaviness come over us once Gryffin was gone, as if he had been a buoyant element that kept us all afloat. The days were filled with more drudgery; it was easier to be irritable. The cascade of joys that had poured over the Parmer Arms came more sparingly now, at a more ordinary rate, and were mixed in with the usual complement of unpleasant events. Nothing too miserable, but nothing too ecstatic, either. Just common life.

Despite Josh's worst fears, business did not entirely slack off at the Arms once Gryffin was gone. Oh, certainly, the pilgrims who came to Thrush Hollow just to meet the Dream-Maker were scarcer now, though there were still plenty of folk who dropped by out of curiosity to see where Gryffin had once lived. And many travelers had simply gotten in the habit of changing horses in Thrush Hollow, and they did not alter their routines even though Gryffin was gone. The expanded dining room and inn still were full about a third of the time, and business remained steady.

Sarah and Bo were married just as fall folded over into winter, and it was the high point of the season for all of us connected to the Arms. Juliet traveled in from Merendon and Raymond from Wodenderry. Gryffin sent a gift with Raymond since he was not strong enough to make the journey himself. Emily and I acted as bridesmaids and carried bouquets of holly and truelove vines. The newlyweds were gone for a week on their honeymoon and returned looking as if they had discovered the answers to the mysteries of the world. I suspected Jack Parmer would be next to marry. Emily, it turned out, was due to have a baby in the spring. So even without the Dream-Maker there to grant our wishes, we learned we could still expect blessings, and gradually we grew reconciled to Gryffin's absence.

Or at least the others did. I did not. I missed him every day. I felt a blankness always at the edge of my vision, an incompleteness to my thoughts. I wrote him every few days and received letters back from him even more often. At the end of each note he always, without fail, printed the words, "I have not forgotten you." Often I looked for this reassurance before I even read the salutation. I told myself that if he ever failed to write that line, I would take it as a sign; I would not go to Wodenderry after all. I would know that my deepest fears had been realized, that he had moved beyond me, and I would not trouble him by appearing at his side like some unwelcome ghost from his past.

But he never forgot. He never failed.

A few days before Wintermoon, he sent a package from Wodenderry, filled with small trinkets for each of us to bind to the wreath. To Emily and Randal he sent a tiny rattle filled with birdseed—and a larger one that they could keep when the baby arrived. To Sarah and Bo, he sent exotic dried fruits—some to attach to the wreath to symbolize prosperity, the rest to eat.

To me he sent a miniature and beautifully carved representation of the queen's palace, complete with minuscule flags flying from the petite turrets. Since he had to have realized I would never burn anything so exquisite, he also sent me a small wagon wheel, obviously pulled from a child's toy. The message was obvious. He expected me to travel to the royal city.

I tied the wheel to the wreath and watched as Josh and his sons tossed the big circle of greenery into the hungry fire. I wondered if your wishes were even more likely to come true if a Dream-Maker wished them for you.

But winter came cruelly and brought sickness with it. Half the town was shut down at one time or another, and there were days we had only a handful of customers at the Arms. That was lucky for me, because I spent two weeks unable to work my shifts. My mother fell violently ill, and for three days I was sure she would not survive. I closed the house to visitors while I nursed her around the clock. Her skin was so hot that I thought her fever might blister her flesh; she succumbed to delirium. Even after the fever broke, her mind wandered and her sentences sometimes made no sense. She did not want to eat and distrusted the liquids I tried to convince her to drink.

"It's just tea, Mother, it will do you good," I would say. Or, "Try a little broth. You need to get your strength back."

"It'll make me forget," she replied once in a croaking voice. "Then they'll trick me."

"Who will trick you?"

"*They* will. They'll tell me lies."

I spooned some soup into her mouth, and she reluctantly swallowed. "I'm the only one here, and I never bother to lie," I said.

"And they'll take him," she said.

I wiped her chin with a napkin. "I don't think they will. That was good, you swallowed some soup. Will you take some more?"

Obediently, she took another spoonful, and then another. "You're so kind to me," she said.

I felt some guilt at that, for I wasn't feeling kind. I was feeling impatient and trapped and desperate to get away. But she was too sick to leave behind. "I want you to get well," I said.

She grabbed my wrist with one of her hot, thin hands, pulling at my arm so strongly that I almost spilled the bowl. "If I'm good, will you tell me?" she asked in a pitiful voice. "If I eat every bite?"

"I'll tell you anyway, even if you don't eat anything," I said. "What do you want to know?"

"Where is he?" she whispered. "What have they done with my son?"

She was disoriented, I told myself. She had forgotten herself, forgotten her own story; it was the fever talking. The sickness had taken her all the way back to her other great illness, more than fifteen years ago when I was born. But I felt such bitterness when I realized that she did not recognize me, as I sat beside her doing my best to keep her alive. That she did not acknowledge me as her daughter. Probably could not have told me my name. In her hour of greatest desperation, she did not call on me. She did not even know who I was.

The sickness passed, and winter finally grew too exhausted to torment us any longer. Spring gamboled in, petulant and charming by turns. Emily had a baby girl and straightaway said she wanted another. Randal's father and sister came to Thrush Hollow, having left the household in secret, to make themselves acquainted with the newest addition to their family.

"If you write your mother," Randal's father said to him, "if you ask her, she will forgive you now, I think. It has been so long, and she misses you so much."

Randal tossed his baby in the air and caught her as she squealed with laughter. "I have done nothing for which I need forgiveness," he said. "I won't ask for it. But *she* should ask it of me."

His father watched him, sadness on the face that looked so much like his son's. "That's not the way the world works," he said.

"I don't much care for how the world works outside of Thrush Hollow," Randal replied. "I am happy here."

Emily's was not the only baby born to my small circle that season. One day a few weeks later, during the rainiest season imaginable, a young woman who was very close to term came to my mother's house seeking a bed for the night.

"It might be a bed for two or three nights," the woman said as she gratefully lowered herself onto the mattress in the guest room. "I'm not sure I can travel any farther. I think—I believe the baby is coming any day now."

I had to wonder if my mother had any memories of her own lying-in, when she had been alone and some distance from home as she was overtaken by labor pains. "Is there anyone I can send for?" my mother asked. "Your husband or your parents?"

The pregnant woman shook her head. "They are all so far away," she said. "I don't think any of them can help me now."

Her name was Anna, or so she said. I thought it was obvious she was concealing secrets, and her name might be only one of them. For one thing, I didn't believe she had a husband, and I had to wonder if, like Emily, she had been a maid servant who caught the attention of a wealthy man. But that only made me feel sorry for her. I fetched her a pail of heated water so she could sponge off the grime of travel, and I made sure she had a glass of warm milk before she went to bed.

And in the middle of the night when she woke us screaming, I ran to fetch the midwife. My mother bustled about the kitchen, pleased rather than not at the midnight turmoil, excited by the idea of ushering a new life into the world. The labor went more speedily than some I had heard of, and by the time dawn came in golden splinters through the bedroom window, Anna had delivered herself of a baby boy.

"What will you call him?" my mother asked as she cuddled the swathed baby in her arms while the midwife cleaned Anna up.

"I don't know," Anna replied in an exhausted voice. "I haven't been able to settle on a name."

The midwife patted Anna's stomach, said, "You were built to have babies," and packed her battered bag.

"How soon can I travel?" Anna asked her.

The midwife shrugged. "Soon as you want. But you might not feel up to it for a day or two."

"I need to get home," Anna said.

"You can stay as long as you like," my mother said. She was still holding the baby, and whispering silly things in his tiny curled ears. "But you sleep now. Kellen and I will watch the little one."

Actually, my mother watched the newborn while I took my shift at the Parmer Arms. When I returned that night, nothing had changed: Anna was still sleeping, and my mother was still holding the infant boy. Eventually Anna roused long enough to eat a light dinner and nurse her son, then returned to her bed. The exertions of the night had worn us all out, and my mother and I were asleep not an hour after Anna was.

In the morning, Anna was gone, offering no note, no coin in payment. She had left her son behind.

I spent a day trying to track down where Anna might have gone, making inquiries at the Arms and the stables and the inn and anywhere else that catered to travelers. But no one could offer me any information about a driver who had taken up a lone woman in the middle of the night. I couldn't believe she could have gotten far on foot, and for another two days I worried that she might be found dead on the road. If she was, word never got back to Thrush Hollow.

There remained the question of what to do with the baby boy.

The whole town knew of his abandonment at our house, of course, and various neighbors dropped by to bring blankets and infant clothing. The woman two doors down, who had just weaned her own twins, was happy to serve as wet nurse and earn a few extra coins. My mother showed the baby off like some exotic trinket purchased at a shop in Merendon. Though I advised against it, she bestowed a name upon him, calling him Georgie after her father's father. More times than I could count in the following days, I came across her with her nose brushing against his nose, cooing to him where he lay in a borrowed cradle. "Hey, Georgie, how's my boy? How's my little baby . . . ?"

It was another week before I realized she intended to keep him.

I had not had much luck finding a foster family. The people I knew and trusted, like Emily and Sarah, were too busy with their own lives, and my mother vetoed most of the others who seemed willing. "That house is filthy. I wouldn't send a dog to live there. . . . She's a fine wet nurse, but she's already got five children, can she really handle another? . . . I don't think he brings in enough money to be able to afford to feed another mouth. . . ." No one was good enough for little Georgie. No one except my mother.

"You seriously think you have the time and energy to raise a baby?" I demanded the night she confessed her desire. "And run a household and entertain the occasional paying guest?"

"I do. Kellen, I really do. Samantha is thirteen now, a very responsible girl, and she's told me she'll work full-time from now on. You're gone so much, I know I can't expect much help from you. But Samantha lives next door and can be here in the middle of the night if I need her. We've had such a successful few years that I've got a good bit of money saved, so even if I turn away customers now and then, I won't be hurting for funds. And—I want him. His mother left him with me. It's like I'm supposed to have him."

Just then Georgie gave a demanding little cry. My mother picked him up and rocked him against her chest. "Isn't that right, Georgie?" she crooned down into his scowling face. "I'm supposed to have you. My baby, my sweet little darling boy . . ."

And then I understood. This was the boy child she had wanted for almost sixteen years; this was the changeling's replacement. I had been wrong, all those times, when I thought her secret desire was to see my father again—that had not been the wish she entrusted to the Dream-Maker, after all. She had whispered, "Give me a son," and her wish had been granted. She finally had what she had always wanted.

Two days later I had packed everything I owned and was on my way to Wodenderry.

Part

Three

Chapter Eighteen

hitched a ride with Ayler, who happened to be passing through Thrush Hollow on his way to Wodenderry. He was patient through the tearful good-byes as I said farewell to everyone at the Parmer Arms, and quiet during the first two hours of the trip, as I sat beside him and tried not to be depressed. I had never been outside of Thrush Hollow in my life, and I almost felt as if I was ripping off a layer of skin as I left the town behind.

But gradually I was possessed by a sense of excitement as well as intense curiosity about the land we were passing through. Ayler, an inveterate wanderer, pointed out interesting sights we encountered, bade me watch the changeover in vegetation as we headed south, and told me the names of the small towns we stopped at. During the four days of the trip, we stopped quite often. Sometimes we would merely get something to drink at the posting house; other times we would have a leisurely lunch or dinner before taking a room for the night at a boardinghouse or an inn. Still other times we would just stroll once through the market square, nodding at people who glanced our way, and then move on.

The point, of course, was to allow anyone with a secret a chance to come up to Ayler and whisper in his ear. The Safe-Keeper was a familiar figure in many of these hamlets, I soon learned. Whether or not people wished to unburden themselves, they were always pleased to see him. The tavern-keeper would not take his money; the posting houses brought us meals for free. We always paid for our beds at night, but at a greatly reduced rate. While I was with him, I was accorded Ayler's status. No one told me secrets, but everyone welcomed my presence.

While I was with him, everyone wondered why.

"So, Ayler, found yourself a girl, have you?" an elderly man asked at our very first stop on our very first day.

"No, she's just a friend. I've known her since she was quite little."

An appraising look, then a shrug. "Well, that's your own secret," he said. "What'll you be drinking today?"

Some version of this conversation occurred at every stop that entire day. If Ayler was as disturbed by the questions as I was, he gave no sign. But, early the next morning, halfway between towns, he obediently pulled the mare to a halt when I said I wanted to take a short break on the side of the road. He fed the horse an apple while I disappeared into the brush.

When I returned, I had exchanged my flat shoes and dress for scuffed boots, loose black trousers, and a long white shirt with the tails hanging out. I had settled a bulky vest over my shoulders to camouflage the shape of my body. I also had pulled back my long hair and tied it with a bit of leather. I knew from experience that anyone who inspected me casually would think I was a boy.

Ayler's inspection was pensive as always. "So you think that's the best disguise to wear as we continue our journey?" he asked, no inflection in his voice.

I shrugged. "It's easiest. Fewer questions."

"And when you arrive in Wodenderry?"

"I had always intended to search for work dressed as a young man," I said, climbing into the wagon and settling on the bench. "I don't know how safe the royal city is for young women on their own."

Ayler settled next to me and slapped the reins. The horse started forward at her usual phlegmatic pace. "Depends on where you go. What kind of work do you think you'll look for?"

I turned my head a little to watch the passing countryside, which seemed to turn even more greenly lush as we proceeded. It was the very beginning of summer, only a breath or two past spring. It had not escaped my notice that yet another chapter of my life was about to open in the golden season. "What I know is inns and restaurants. There must be plenty of those in Wodenderry, and one or two must have work for willing hands."

"Indeed. And I know of a place—" Ayler began, and lapsed into silence. This was habitual with him as he considered a new thought; it might be five minutes between one of his sentences and the next. I waited. "Actually, it might do very well," he finally continued. "It's a tavern, rather small, but extremely charming. Run by a young woman named Leona who is"—he glanced at me—"perhaps ten years older than you."

"And she runs a tavern on her own?" I said. "That's unusual."

Ayler nodded. "It was her father's. He died a couple of years ago, leaving the place to her. To a point, she's been successful, but I think the work is harder than she thought—and there are a lot of taverns in Wodenderry. Hers is not always as full as she would like."

"She might not be able to pay me anything if she doesn't have any customers," I pointed out.

"Indeed. But I think you might be able to work out a deal with her. Some of your salary to be paid in room and board. You will be safe at Leona's as you might not be in some other parts of town, or other residences. And she need not fear that you will run off with the silver or steal from the till, because I will vouch for you. Actually, you would be doing her a kindness if you went to work for her. She needs the help of someone she can trust. And those sorts of people are sometimes rare in the royal city."

"All right. I'll meet her," I said. "And if I like her and she wants me, I'll stay."

"This might work very well," he said again.

We traveled for a few more moments in silence—although it was never entirely silent in Ayler's wagon. I had noticed that on our first day. It was the creakiest cart imaginable, the wood of its frame popping and screeching even when we passed over utterly smooth terrain. If you shifted your weight ever so minutely on the bench, the boards groaned in protest, and the wheels clattered even as they followed soft, deep ruts in dry dirt roads.

"Why is your cart so noisy?" I demanded as we squealed through a crossroads at a sedate pace.

Ayler laughed. "It's built of chatterleaf wood. Very loud. I sometimes think, even at night in the barn when the wagon's not moving at all, the boards are probably whispering and conversing with one another, making their own special racket."

I stared at him. "Why would a Safe-Keeper build a cart from chatterleaf trees?" I asked. "Those are for Truth-Tellers."

Ayler nodded. "I know. And for a year or two I drove through the kingdom in a cart made of kirrenberry timbers. Never mind how rough the road, that cart never made a sound. I found I did not like it. I am not used to silence." He glanced down at me, read the surprise in my face, and smiled. "Truly, I am not. *I* am not the most talkative man, perhaps, but others are always speaking to me, telling me their stories. I find, even if it's only metal and wood, I still want to hear the voices."

"You're the strangest man," I commented.

Ayler gave a low laugh. "Aren't we all strange," he countered, "in our own ways?"

We reached Wodenderry a few hours after noon on the fifth day. Never had I seen such a place! I sat rapt on the bench

as Ayler negotiated the narrow streets, thick with traffic—
pedestrians, solitary horses, grand carriages pulled by
matched teams, humbler carts like ours. Looming over us
from both sides were closely packed buildings of wood and
stone, most of them two stories high. Some were beautiful,
built of a dense silver-hued marble and decorated with flags
and flower boxes; others were plain and mean and grimed
with soot. Vendors stood on almost every corner, selling
everything from bread to housewares to shoes. The noise
was loud and incessant—people shouting, horses whicker-
ing, wagon wheels clanging against metal grates in the road.
It was both terrifying and wonderful. I felt assaulted by energy; my mind began to hum. I wondered how anyone ever
relaxed enough to fall asleep in Wodenderry.

After I had been silent for a few minutes, Ayler glanced
down at me. "A little overwhelming, isn't it?" he said. "You'll
grow used to it, though. You'll even find, when you leave,
that you start to crave it. Wodenderry gets a hold on your
senses and doesn't let go."

"I would think you could get so lost here that no one
could ever find you again."

"You could," Ayler agreed, "if you wanted to." He carefully navigated his way around a wagon stopped at the side
of the road. "But who wants to be lost?"

About half an hour after we had entered the city, Ayler
turned down a quieter street and pulled the cart into an
alley. We had come to rest beside a one-and-a-half-story
structure built of gray stone, roofed with orange tile, and
taking advantage of a very small square of lawn to sprout a

vivid array of flowers. On the front of the building, as we had passed, I had noticed a weathered sign painted with the word COTTLESON'S in block letters.

"It's safe to leave the mare here for a few minutes," Ayler said. "Let's go in and meet Leona."

I understood the hospitality trade, so I knew we had arrived at a good time, midway between lunch and the evening hour when people would begin drifting in for a glass of ale. Even so, I noticed a few customers in place as we pushed through the thick front door and entered. The room was smaller than the dining hall at the Parmer Arms, but appealing, with dark beams set against a whitewashed ceiling, a cluster of tables arranged in the middle of the room, booths lining the two side walls, and a highly polished bar at the back. Lighting was supplied by half a dozen stained-glass windows, shaded lanterns at each table, and an array of candles behind the bar. I could smell the comforting and familiar scents of yeast, onions, meat, and ale. Not so strange in Wodenderry after all.

A door behind the bar swung open, and a young woman stepped through, bearing a tray. She was about my height and wore a plain gray gown. Her drab dress and her rather severe coiffure didn't do much to disguise the gorgeous color of her hair—a dark auburn—and her rather anxious expression could not conceal the lovely contours of her heart-shaped face. She glanced at us just enough to acknowledge our existence, then carried her burden to one of the occupied booths, where she had a short conversation with the two men sitting there. Then, wiping her hands on her apron, she approached us.

"Yes? Would you like—*Ayler*! I didn't realize it was you!" she exclaimed, and threw her arms around the Safe-Keeper. "It is so good to see you! I thought you were traveling the rest of the season."

"And so I am, but my travels have brought me here," Ayler replied. "I thought I would check on you since I am in Wodenderry. How is life since I saw you last?"

The woman grimaced and pushed at a lock of hair that had strayed from confinement. "Much the same, but even more hectic," she confessed. "Jedlo quit—going back to the farm—so now I am down to just me and Sallie, and there is more *work* to be done than two women can finish in a day. Phillip comes and goes as he pleases, and is more trouble than help, frankly, and there are days I think—oh, well." She attempted a smile. "But you did not come here just to hear my complaining. Are you hungry? When did you arrive?"

"Yes, and just now," Ayler replied. "But let me first introduce you to a young man I have brought with me all the way from Thrush Hollow. He wanted to see the royal city, and he is feeling quite awestruck. Kellen, meet Leona Cottleson, our harried hostess. Leona, this is Kellen Carmichael."

Leona bestowed a friendly smile on me. "I've never been to Thrush Hollow, but if it's as small as the towns where I grew up, then I understand your amazement at arriving in the city," she said. "But I love Wodenderry now! I could not imagine living anywhere else."

"My thought was to stay and make it my home as well,"

I said, consciously using the lowest register of my voice. Still, she would think me a lad of fourteen, perhaps, beardless and slim. I would turn sixteen in a few weeks, but I knew that I seemed younger as a boy.

"And do your parents have an opinion about your moving to the royal city?" Leona asked. "Or are they no longer alive?"

"Living, but uninterested," I replied.

She nodded, complete understanding on her face. "Mine are both dead now, but it hardly makes a difference," she said. "Well, I miss my father." She glanced around the tavern with affection. "He built this place, and we ran it together for several years. That was the only time I ever felt close to him." She brought her gaze back to my face. "So what do you plan to do in Wodenderry, Kellen? I assume you're looking for work?"

"Yes. I had a job at the Parmer Arms in Thrush Hollow," I said, answering carefully. It would not do to say, *I have been a servant girl* or *a maid.* "I worked in the kitchen and waited on customers and did the gardening or the chopping when an extra hand was needed. I also helped my mother, who ran a temporary boardinghouse. I am used to the work done at a place like yours."

"What Kellen means is that I thought you might offer him a place," Ayler interposed. "I know he can do the work, and I know you need the hands."

Leona looked hopeful. "Oh, indeed I do! But—as Ayler might also have told you—I don't know how well I can pay anyone. Business has been slow—"

"As you might have surmised, Kellen has nowhere else to go," Ayler said gently. "A bed and the promise of a few meals would almost be adequate salary."

"Now *that* I could offer him," Leona said. "A small bed, it's true, but a bed."

I laughed. "At my mother's, for most of the last few years, I have slept on a mat in the kitchen," I said. "I don't ask for much more."

Leona smiled. "I can do slightly better than that. There's only one bedroom upstairs, and that's mine, but I have always kept the room off the kitchen for Phillip. However, he's not sleeping there anymore. He has taken up with friends who are somewhat older and who have quarters down by the docks. Not very reputable friends, I might add. In any case, the room is empty."

"Who's Phillip?" I asked. In my experience, dispossessed people often did not like to be dispossessed, and I wanted to know a little about him before he came back to reclaim his place.

Leona made a sour face. "My brother."

"Her scapegrace brother," Ayler amended. "You'll meet him, no doubt, for he has a tendency to show up when it's least convenient."

"Demanding things I cannot give him, and complaining bitterly about how badly he is treated," Leona added. "Such a joy in my life is Phillip."

We seemed to have strayed from the main point. I took a deep breath. "Then," I said, "if his room is empty and you need the help and you will trust me to work for you, will you hire me?"

"Oh! I thought we had already settled that! Yes, of course I will," she responded. She glanced at the Safe-Keeper. "If Ayler recommends you, you know, I cannot help but trust you. In fact, I like you already."

Ayler's face was touched with his usual abstracted smile. "Yes," he said in a dreamy voice, "I think this will work out very well."

Chapter Nineteen

loved working at Cottleson's. From the very beginning, the place felt familiar to me. Perhaps it was because I knew the work, although running a tavern was somewhat different from either a posting house or a bed-and-breakfast. But there were still meals to prepare, customers to please, cash boxes to balance, and various chores of maintenance and upkeep to complete.

Perhaps it was because Leona reminded me a little of Sarah Parmer. Well, in fact, she was nothing like Sarah. Where Sarah was serene and a little stately, Leona could be passionate and quick to show temper. But they were both warm-hearted women a few years older than I was. They were both kind to me when I needed kindness. They were both grateful for the gifts I brought and always thinking of ways to turn those to good use. So for Leona, as for Sarah, I accomplished a wide range of tasks. While Leona and Sallie mostly waited on customers, I became the primary cook and keeper of the kitchen. I also shopped for food in the market, tended the minuscule garden out back, haggled

with peddlers when they came to the door, and fought a per-
petual war with vermin.

One day I became the unofficial protector of the other
women under the roof.

It was nighttime, actually, not far from midnight, and
the tavern was almost empty. I was in the kitchen, scrub-
bing the last of the pans, when I heard a commotion from
the front room. There was a squeal, then a round of laughter, then the sound of Leona's raised voice, both furious and
fearful. I dropped the pan, grabbed a poker from the fire-
place, and ran through the swinging door to investigate.

Sallie was struggling in the embrace of a drunken fellow
whose two companions were exhorting him to *kiss 'er, kiss
'er good, that's a pretty girl, Bart.* Sallie was shrieking and
Leona was circling the intertwined couple, still shouting,
her raised hands pounding at the back and shoulders of
Sallie's captor. As I entered, one of the other men still seated
in the booth grabbed Leona's arm and yanked her onto his
lap. She tumbled toward him so hard her feet flew up to
reveal a froth of petticoats.

I charged in. One hard swing of the poker caught Sallie's
attacker in the back of the head, causing him to yelp,
release her, and go staggering across the room. Surprise
made the other man release Leona, and she leapt to her
feet, red-faced and raging.

"Out of here! All of you, out of here! And never come
back!" she cried.

"Here, now, you can't be hitting people on the head,"
the man in the booth said, giving me a darkling look.

"You're next if you don't get up and get out, like she says," I threatened, brandishing my weapon. I knew I didn't look particularly menacing—I appeared so young, so soft—but I figured they were drunk and I was a lot stronger than they knew. I could take them, at least one by one.

"Kellen!" Sallie shrieked, and I whirled around just in time to see the first man launch an assault on me. I didn't hesitate. I kicked him in the groin, hard, a move Ayler had taught me many years ago. He grunted and went down. I returned my attention to the men in the booth, no longer laughing.

"Out," I said grimly. "And take your friend with you."

They blustered some more, but soon found that Leona had armed herself, too, snatching up another poker since mine had worked so well. Spitting invective and insults, they gathered up their friend and hauled him through the front door. I glanced around, ascertained that they were the last customers for the day, and locked the door behind them.

Leona had collapsed at one of the tables in the middle of the room and looked wan and exhausted. Sallie, a strapping blonde girl of about nineteen, seemed none the worse for wear. I imagined this hadn't been the first time she'd been the unwilling recipient of an overeager kiss. She bustled back behind the bar and drew glasses of ale for each of us. We settled around the table with Leona.

"Does this sort of thing happen often?" I asked.

Leona shook her head, then nodded. "Never when my father was here. Sometimes since he's been gone. Men think they can take advantage of women."

"Usually I just give them the knee," Sallie said. "But he caught me when I wasn't paying attention, and I couldn't get free." She toasted me with her glass and gave me a warm smile. "Glad you were here, Kellen. Very heroic to have a boy like you come to my rescue."

I spared a moment to hope she didn't start to think I was a romantic prospect, and then I decided that I was too young and slender to appeal to Sallie. I had seen the men she liked to flirt with, and they were all hardy and full of muscles.

"Is it better when Phillip's around?" I asked. I had been here two weeks and had yet to meet the reprobate brother.

Leona shrugged. "Phillip brings his own trouble. His friends are just as likely to cause a ruckus as to save you from one once it's started." She nodded at me. "But I too am glad you were here, Kellen. You're tougher than you look."

I grinned. "I guess we're all full of surprises."

"Maybe you should walk Sallie home," Leona suggested. "If those men were angry, and they've decided to lie in wait—"

"Happy to," I said.

Sallie shook her head and rose to her feet. "I'll slip out the back way. It's only two streets, and my father waits up till I'm home. Anyone comes after me tonight, he'll get more than a poker to the head if my father catches him."

"Good night, then," Leona said and yawned. "I'm so tired. I'll see you both in the morning."

Sallie survived the walk home, and we had only minor incidents like that in the days that followed. But I could tell that my very presence made Leona and Sallie feel safer, and I rather relished the idea of being a champion. I had always liked being strong enough to defend myself, to fight for and keep my own place in the world. It was novel but agreeable to think I might be called upon to fight for someone else as well.

I had been in Wodenderry three weeks before I saw Gryffin.

I thought about him every day—heard about him at least as often. It was Sallie who took it upon herself to tell me what she clearly considered his romantic tale. We were working all day to clean up after a late but fairly well-behaved Summermoon celebration the night before.

"There he was, this crippled boy, living in one of those small towns that nobody ever goes to, everyone being mean to him! His whole life! And then one day a Truth-Teller comes to town and says, 'Melinda's power has faded but I see it has come to rest in *you*.' And so Ayler brings him to Wodenderry, and he goes to live with the queen. And every day he has an audience, in this enormous room just filled with people, and he comes rolling in—he's in a wheeled chair, you know—and he talks to everybody for a few minutes. They say sometimes there are two hundred people there, and he talks to every single one."

"And how many of their wishes come true?" I asked.

"Oh, I don't know about that. Sometimes the magic takes its own time. But they do say he's the most powerful Dream-Maker anyone can remember. People can feel a tingle if he touches them with his hands."

Gryffin had touched me more than once, and I hadn't

felt any tingle. "I doubt that many people remember a Dream-Maker before Melinda," I replied rather tartly. "She held the office a long time."

"Do you have any wishes?" Sallie asked. "You ought to go see him."

"Have you been?"

She nodded. "Once or twice. I can't say my wishes came true, but I felt better just being in the room with him. Hopeful. Like something good might happen."

Yes, that was a feeling I could confirm. I had always felt hopeful in Gryffin's presence, capable of almost anything. "Maybe I'll go see him," I said. "Someday soon."

I knew he would be hurt to learn I had been in Wodenderry so long without seeking him out. He had written me several times since I had left Thrush Hollow, and Sarah had forwarded his letters. I had written back brief notes that didn't say much. The truth was, I was deeply afraid. A year was a long time to go without seeing someone, especially someone whose life had undergone such a radical change. He could not have become more strange and powerful if he had been named king; he could not have seemed more inaccessible to a country girl come to the city in disguise. He still closed all his letters with the phrase "I have not forgotten you." But I thought that might be a way to comfort himself by clinging to a familiar past that made the demanding present seem a little less strange. He might not have forgotten me, but he might not have remembered me as I really was.

Still, I had come to Wodenderry to see him. So I would

see him. Sallie drew me a map to the palace and I walked there one morning, staring around me like a yokel newly arrived from a coastal town. Since my arrival in Wodenderry, I had not strayed far from Cottleson's and the streets that took me to the markets and back. I was impressed by the fine houses and expensive shops that crowded so close to the palace grounds. The palace itself left me speechless, with its wide sweep of lawn, its parade of soldiers, its grand architecture. I couldn't imagine my Gryffin living here. I couldn't imagine *anyone* living here.

A few mumbled phrases to the guards at the gate and the front door got me escorted to a huge, high-ceilinged room that seemed to be toward the rear of the palace. I found a place in the very back of the room, behind a row of travelers who had spread blankets on the floor and were feeding their children a sloppy lunch. I counted maybe fifty people there before me, and more arrived in ones and twos over the next thirty minutes. Someone had attempted to make the room seem a little less imposing by fitting it with benches and chairs, decorating it with flowers, and installing three small fountains where people could splash up water to drink or cool their faces. Still, it was high summer, and the room was hot. Both flowers and visitors wilted as they waited.

I had been there almost an hour when Gryffin arrived. Excitement swept over the crowd like a breeze across a cornfield. The room rippled as everyone stood up, first those in front, then those in the middle, then those of us in back. Past all the heads and bodies, I could catch only a glimpse of Gryffin, but I strained and contorted to try to get a better look. He was sitting in a customized chair that looked finer than the one Bo had built him, with bigger spoked wheels that he could obviously manipulate himself. He didn't need to, however. He entered the room accompanied by two soldiers and an attendant, who propelled the chair from behind. I was too far away to get a really good look at Gryffin's face, but what I saw made my chest hurt and my cheeks flush. He was so familiar, so dear. He wore an expression of kind seriousness, like a man charged with a delicate task that he had promised himself to perform extremely well. He was dressed in clothes that even from a distance looked expensive and well made, and his hair had been fashionably cut, but none of that really mattered. He still looked like Gryffin.

"Form a line!" one of the guards bawled out. "The Dream-Maker will speak to each of you in turn!"

I hung back, as did some of the unwieldy families with multiple children, but most everyone else rushed forward. Soon a ragged line was snaking around the room as people waited their chance to entrust Griffin with their wishes. It didn't seem that Gryffin talked to any one person very long, for the line moved forward at a fairly brisk pace. What was there to say to him, really? *Heal my husband. Find my daughter. Introduce me to my own true love.* How complex were most people's desires? Couldn't the majority of them be summed up in a sentence or two?

I hovered at the back of the room, trying to get up my courage to approach, trying to frame the words to my own wish. *Be my friend still.* Not the sort of thing to say out loud,

I thought. At least, I couldn't do it. But perhaps the words would not need to be spoken. Perhaps Gryffin would glance up, see my face, and show a deep and sudden gladness. He would wave me over and send the guards away and exclaim, "Kellen! I have missed you so much!"

But he did not look up. He did not feel the pull of my insistent gaze. He kept his attention courteously on whichever supplicant stood before him, detailing specific and surely insignificant desires.

I should not have come here. Maybe not to Wodenderry, definitely not to the palace. I could not bring myself to ask for the Dream-Maker's attention.

I drifted over to stand near a large family that was just now packing up their baskets and blankets, and I followed them as they exited the audience room. The children dashed up and down the palace hallways till frowned into decorum by posted guards. The parents talked with great animation about the magical experience of meeting the Dream-Maker, and, oh, wouldn't it be lovely if the wishes really did come true? I trudged along behind them in silence, feeling sad and sick. Ready to give up on dreams altogether.

Chapter Twenty

ack at Cottleson's, I found I was not the only one whose day was going badly. Sallie looked harassed and irritable as I stepped through the front door. It was afternoon, but there were half a dozen tables full of customers, and she seemed to be handling them all by herself.

"Where's Leona?" I asked, and Sallie jerked her chin toward my domain.

"In the kitchen. With *Phillip.* Fine mood she's in, too."

I raised my eyebrows, but I was aware of more interest than apprehension. Finally a chance to meet the elusive and disagreeable brother.

I pushed through the swinging door into the kitchen to find Leona in a pose of tense confrontation with a young man who could only be Phillip. He was tall and gangly, with dirty blond hair and a sullen demeanor. He was quite a few years younger than Leona, maybe sixteen or seventeen, and he looked nothing like her in coloring or bone structure. All they seemed to have in common at this particular moment were expressions of bitterness.

They both pivoted to stare at me as I stepped into the room. Neither of them looked welcoming. "Sorry," I said, my hand still on the door. "Should I go?"

"Who's that?" the young man said, ready to pounce. "Is that the stranger you've put in my place?"

"That's Kellen, yes," Leona replied evenly. "But it's hardly your *place* since you left it months ago and have showed no interest in coming back."

He turned back toward her, his dark eyes bright with malice. "Whether I'm here every night or gone for the next five years, I have an interest in the business," he said. "Half of it's mine, don't you forget that. Maybe more than half. That's what Barney says."

"I've done the work. I've paid for the upkeep. I've kept the whole place *running*, and you think any of it is *yours*?" Leona demanded. The words sounded well worn, as if she had uttered them many times before and rehearsed them over and over silently in her mind. "I've told you before, you're welcome to sleep here, to eat here, anytime you want. But the tavern belongs to me."

"We'll see about that, won't we?" Phillip taunted. "Barney says—"

"Barney can keep his stupid, drunken words to himself," Leona shot back. "What *Barney* doesn't know about inheritance and law—"

Phillip spun on his heel and hit the back door hard, causing it to jangle open. "He knows more than you think," he said in an ominous voice. "I'll be coming back.

This isn't done yet." And he stalked out and disappeared.

Leona stood for a moment, her whole body a study in frustrated rage, then sank with a little moan to a stool set by the large kitchen table. She rested her head in her hands and seemed ready to start crying.

"I don't know what that was all about," I said cautiously. "But—"

"I hate him," she said, her voice muffled by her hands. "I know you shouldn't say that about your brother, but I do. I *hate* him. He's never been anything but miserable and greedy and unkind and relentless." She raised her head and looked at me with an unseeing gaze. "He was born ten years after I was. It was all my mother could talk about. 'I have a son, I finally have a son.' It was as if I had stopped to exist, after ten years, because I was only a daughter. Was your mother like that?"

I hardly knew how to answer. "Yes," I said finally. "I never would have pleased her if I had been born a girl."

"I don't understand it." Leona dropped her head to her hands again. "So, as you can imagine, he was much indulged, and he became the most unlikable child imaginable. At least I thought so—he's always had friends, of a sort, despicable people like this Barney fellow. They just encourage all his worst traits, and now he's—he's—"

"It sounds like he wants to fight you for possession of the tavern," I said.

She nodded, still staring down at the table. "That's what he came for tonight. He wants me to sell the tavern, take his half of the money, and invest it in some dreadful scheme of Barney's. Which you know can only lead to disaster! I told him I wouldn't do it, and now he's threatening to try to take the business away from me altogether."

"Can he do that?"

"I don't know. My father said he left it to me. I can inherit it, can't I, all of it? A father can leave property to one child and not another, can't he?"

"I don't know," I said. "Maybe you need a lawyer."

She made a sound that was halfway between a laugh and another groan. "I can't afford one. Oh, Kellen, we're barely making it as it is. I don't know, maybe Phillip's right. Maybe I should sell the place." She looked up again, and her eyes were red with tears. "This was always my dream," she whispered. "To run a business of my own. I love Wodenderry. I love this place. What will I do if I have to sell it?"

I put a hand on her shoulder to comfort her, afraid to hug her as I wanted because she might feel the shape of my body under my vest and guess my secret. "Maybe you should visit the Dream-Maker," I said.

She laughed again, shook her head, and stood up, trying to look calm and determined. "I don't have time to go chasing after my dreams that way," she said. "I just have to work harder. I have to figure out how to stop Phillip. I have to— well, I have to go out there right now and help Sallie. Can you get dinner started? Everyone's hungry."

"Right now," I said, reaching for a head of lettuce. "It will be the best dinner you ever tasted."

She gave me a tremulous smile. "Oh, Kellen, I don't know what I would do without you," she said. "I like you so much better than my own brother."

"Anybody would," I said practically, and she actually laughed. "Try not to worry," I added. "And I'll try to think of something else I can do to help."

Well. What would help most would be to go to the Dream-Maker and lay all our hopes before him. I tried. I did. I went to the palace three more times in the next five days, sure that this time I would be able to overcome my shyness, or my fear, and approach Gryffin. But I couldn't do it. I would know as soon as he saw my face if my own dream might come true, and I suppose I was not ready for such an immediate answer. I went, I watched him, and I walked away. I was so used to being rejected by the person I most wanted to love me that I found myself unable to take the risk. It was preferable not to know. It was preferable to think there was still a chance.

In the end, it was Emily who betrayed me. One too many letters from Gryffin had arrived at the Parmer Arms addressed to me, and she snatched this one away from Sarah before Sarah could forward it on. "She's living in Wodenderry now, at a place called Cottleson's," Emily wrote on the envelope before returning it to the mail coach. "She goes by her own name but she's dressed as a boy."

"It does nobody any good to try to hide," she declared, her hands on her hips. "I should know. I tried it. And I'm so much happier now."

Of course, I didn't learn all this until Sarah's letter reached me, a day after Emily's note made it into Gryffin's hands.

I was working in the kitchen, busy with preparations for the night's meal, when I heard the low murmur of shock and excitement buzz through the outer room. Some locally famous figure, I supposed—one of the wealthy merchants who lived in the city, or maybe even a group of young noblemen, mingling with the common folk as a lark. The room had been only about a quarter full when I'd peeked out a few minutes earlier, which made the cook's task easier but made Leona's burden heavier. How to make a profit from such a thin house? I hoped the noblemen liked my chicken pie, one of my better dishes, and were willing to come back often if it was on the menu.

The door swept back and Leona brushed through, looking utterly bewildered. "Kellen. There's somebody out there. Who says he knows you."

I looked up from my chopping board. "Really? Did he give his name?" It couldn't be Ayler, because Leona would recognize him, but Randal or Bo or one of the Parmer boys could have come to Wodenderry. It would be wonderful to see any of them.

"Did he—no, I don't think he gave his name," Leona answered in a very strange voice. "But why don't you go out and see if you know who he is."

I laid aside my knife, dried my hands, and stepped into the taproom.

To see Gryffin sitting there, his eyes expectantly on the door.

I stood silently for a moment, unable to move, merely staring. Well, of course, everyone was staring at everyone.

The ten or so people in the tavern were all still watching Gryffin. Leona and Sallie were focused on me. Gryffin and I had eyes only for each other. He was seated in the new wheeled chair, pulled up to one of the center tables, his hands folded before him. I thought his face looked a little fuller than it had when he had left Thrush Hollow, though at the same time sharper—as if he was meant by nature to have a round, comfortable face but a year of listening to whispered dreams had whittled away any softness that came from harboring illusions. He knew now the extent of want and desire; he was acquainted with both simple and impossible hopes.

"Gryffin," I whispered, and put a hand to my throat.

"You *are* here," he replied. "Didn't you think I'd want to know?"

"I—" I looked around the room, acutely conscious of a dozen pairs of eyes watching me, everyone wondering how a boy like me had come to know the Dream-Maker. *A boy like me.* I couldn't forget how I was dressed, who I was supposed to be. "I came to the palace. To see you. But you seemed so busy."

"I'm not busy now," he said. "Sit down. We can talk."

"I—" Now I glanced back at the kitchen door, still quivering slightly on its hinges. "I have work to do. I handle the cooking. Maybe later, when I'm done—"

Gryffin nodded. "I'll wait," he said. Unexpectedly, he smiled. It was as if all the stained-glass windows in the tavern suddenly turned to lit jewels; that's how much the room brightened. "I'll have dinner while I wait. I'm hungry."

"Dinner. Right away," I said, and grabbed Leona's arm as I headed back through the kitchen door.

"Kellen!" she exclaimed when we were alone. "How do you know the *Dream-Maker*? Is he a friend of yours? How can that be?"

"He lived in Thrush Hollow when I did," I said briefly. "Leona, go get Sallie's sisters. Get the neighbor girls, or boys, or anyone who can work. You wanted to bring more customers to the tavern? You're going to be busier tonight than you've ever been."

"Why? Because the Dream-Maker is here? I'm not sure anyone even saw him come in."

"It doesn't matter. Trust me. In an hour, you're going to have a line of people out the door. We need help."

She stared a moment longer, and then she laughed. "I'll be back as soon as I can," she said, and flew out the back door.

That was a night none of us ever forgot, Gryffin's first visit to Cottleson's. I was right, of course. Within the hour, the place was packed to overflowing, and patrons lined up patiently on the walk outside. Sallie's sisters helped me in the kitchen, while her younger brother worked the crowd outside, selling drinks and plates of food. The neighbor woman, who ran a millinery shop, was pressed into service to find any vendors who might still be open at this hour, selling raw ingredients or prepared food. I chopped and sliced and kneaded and stirred and baked with such fierce concentration that I hardly felt the hours go by, except that I finally began to slow from dizziness and exhaustion. By that time, it was very late, and we had served hundreds of people.

Leona came staggering through the door, looking dazed but happy. "Go," she said. "I've cleared out the room. Everyone's gone but the Dream-Maker and the guards who came with him, and they're waiting outside. He wants to talk to you."

I looked around the kitchen. "I'll never get this clean," I said.

"We'll do it in the morning. Right now I'm going straight upstairs to bed," she said. "Go visit with your friend."

I washed my hands, smoothed back my hair, and stepped into the tavern to see Gryffin.

He was sitting at the same table, looking almost as tired as I felt, but he smiled when I pulled up a seat. "I enjoyed that," he said. "Much more fun than holding a formal audience. Every third person told me they would never be so bold as to go to the palace so they never thought they'd have a chance to meet me. I should come here once a week, at least."

"Leona would like that," I said. "The business is struggling. But if you were here from time to time—"

He nodded. "I'll do that. I'll go anywhere you are."

He was watching me very closely, but the expression in his eyes was hard to read. I felt myself gulping, trying to swallow an obstruction in my throat. "It seemed so different," I said in a small voice. "When I came to the palace to find you. You seemed—it seemed—there was a place there for you."

"And you didn't think there was a place there for you just because you're my friend?"

"I didn't know what to say. I didn't know what might have changed."

"Nothing's changed," he said instantly.

"I was afraid you might not remember me," I said.

He held his hands out, extending them over the silky wood of the table, and I laid my hands in his. "Kellen," he said. "You were the first person who ever cared about me. Now everyone cares about me, but it is very hard to separate out who wants to be my friend because I might do them a favor, and who wants to be my friend because they like me for who I am. There are days in Wodenderry I have felt more lost and alone and afraid than the day I crawled to your house in a rainstorm with both my legs broken. The only thing that has helped me remember who I am is remembering who *you* are."

"Maybe you're not supposed to remember who you were," I said, "once you become Dream-Maker."

His fingers tightened over mine. His hands had always been so strong. "Maybe it's even more important, once the power comes over you," he replied.

"I missed you so much," I said. "I haven't known how to tell you that."

"I thought about you every day," he replied. He hesitated, and I wondered what he was going to say, and then he laughed. "It's strange to see you dressed as a boy again," he said.

"I thought you never noticed anything I wore. Whether I wore clothes suited to a boy or a girl."

"It never *mattered* to me," he said. "But I usually noticed."

I tried to free my hands from his. "I suppose the Dream-Maker shouldn't be seen holding hands with a young man."

But Gryffin didn't let me go. "And why not, if that's who he feels like holding hands with?" he replied in a quiet voice. His grip tightened again as he pulled me toward him, and I came to my feet and stepped around the edge of the table. I thought Leona was too tired to be watching from the kitchen, and the guards too discreet to be peering through the front window, but if they were, I didn't care. I leaned down and brushed my mouth, very softly, across Gryffin's. He smiled, and I kissed him again, still gently.

"I'm so glad you've found me again, Gryffin," I whispered. "I didn't know how much longer I could go on without you."

Chapter Twenty-One

fter that, Gryffin came to Cottleson's about one evening a week, varying the day of his arrival so no one knew whether he would be there or not. This meant the tavern was always busy, since customers would drop by looking for him, and more often than not stay long enough to have a beer or two before leaving.

Sometimes they stayed because they had heard a rumor: The Dream-Maker occasionally came to the tavern to relax in private, sitting alone in a designated room and declining the chance to visit with the populace. They all respected his wish for solitude, but they also knew that the very presence of a Dream-Maker was enough to confer magic. They knew he could make dreams come true even when they weren't spoken aloud. So they came, they looked around hopefully, they speculated that Gryffin was sitting in austere state in an elegant chamber, and they ordered a pitcher of ale.

In fact, there were a few nights Gryffin *did* come to Cottleson's and *did* remain out of sight—but he wasn't eating a sumptuous meal in a specially reserved room. He was back in the kitchen with me, chopping vegetables and stirring pots and swapping stories. We celebrated my birthday together in Leona's kitchen, not telling the others what day it was because I was sure no one expected a boy my age to make a fuss about such an event. But Gryffin brought me a book and a painted miniature of the queen, and I was happy.

Most of the time, though, we just talked. We had so much to catch up on! I told him about my mother's adoption of the abandoned Georgie and how she was so busy with her new child that she rarely had time to write me. I faithfully sent her money, and always asked after my stepbrother, but I could not count on a regular correspondence. When she wrote, she seemed sublimely happy, though pressed for time. I was sad to say I did not miss her at all.

He told me of his first lonely months in Wodenderry, surrounded by gawking strangers, feeling as if he might be devoured by the intense hungers of the people he had come to serve. "And what I told you the other night was true," he added as he busily wielded his knife on a pile of carrots. "I found it very hard to separate out the friends from the sycophants. For the first few months I was here, the only people I really trusted were the Truth-Tellers. Not always the most pleasant people to be around, but at least I knew they were incapable of pretending to like me if they didn't."

During that time we talked about ourselves but only through a filter, telling the stories of our recent lives by speaking of our changing relationships with other people. Neither of us had forgotten those two shy kisses in the middle of Leona's tavern, but neither of us mentioned them again. I think we did not know the words to say, though if I had tried, I would have said, *I am very sure I love you, but I am just turned sixteen. It seems strange to imagine a life alongside you, but I cannot imagine any other life. You are in my heart, and I cannot believe that you will be uprooted, but perhaps we should live awhile longer before we say we are certain.*

On Gryffin's part, I guessed the words would be much the same if he were to speak them, but I thought he might add another sentence: *Can you really love a man whose body is broken?* I knew the answer, and I hoped he did, but I was fairly certain the question concerned him. Now and then I saw him lean over and rub his twisted calves, then straighten up and glance over at me. His face, at those times, was always sad.

"Do you walk at all anymore?" I asked him one day as we were making soup in the kitchen.

He shook his head. "I can stand, and take a few steps, but it's painful."

"Are your legs getting worse?"

"I think so." He shrugged. "The lot of a Dream-Maker. Suffering and pain. It's nothing I can't endure."

"Do you have someone to massage them for you?"

He laughed. "Yes, the royal physician! Who is a very kind soul. But"—he shook his head—"there is not much improvement. Perhaps as I get older my legs get weaker. I try not to complain. The price seems fair."

"Buying joy for other people?" I said, a skeptical edge to my voice. "It might seem a little steep to me."

He laughed again. "Well, it makes me happy to see people like your friend Leona prosper. So I am rewarded in my way."

Indeed, Leona's prosperity was a satisfaction to all of us. Business had picked up so significantly that Leona hired Sallie's sister full-time to help me in the kitchen, and Sallie's brother to wait on tables. We were all exhausted by the extra work, but elated with the extra money, and Leona paid handsome bonuses to Sallie and me that month.

"Business has been so good that I've managed to pay off the last loan," Leona gloated at the end of one very long day. Sallie had gone home for the night, and Leona and I were drinking a last cup of tea before seeking our beds. "Even if Gryffin stops coming here regularly, we can make it now on the kind of money we used to bring in. Kellen, I do believe your friend has made my dream come true."

I smiled. "That's his job, and he does it well."

She turned her head to consider me. "Although sometimes I think Ayler's the one who really started my run of good fortune, when he brought you here," she said. "You're the best worker I've ever had, even better than Sallie, though of course Sallie's a treasure, too. It's just that you— I don't know. You make things so easy. We get along so well. I know I'm not really old enough to be your mother, but sometimes I feel like I am. Or your aunt, maybe. I want you to do well, and be happy, and marry a nice young girl, and invite me to the wedding, and buy a house next to mine, and bring over each of the babies for my blessing once they're born. Doesn't that sound silly? I guess I've always had such a footloose life up till now that I find myself wanting to hold on to the things I value—this tavern, the few friends I've made. I don't want to let go of anyone. I hate the thought of you going back to Thrush Hollow sometime."

I shook my head, my throat too tight for me to speak at first. "I don't think I'll be returning to Thrush Hollow anytime soon," I said at last. "It certainly won't be family ties that pull me back. I wasn't sure I wanted to come to Wodenderry, but I love it here. I love the tavern. I can't think of anyplace else I'd rather work or people I'd rather be with."

"Well, someday you might want a bigger place to live," she said practically. "And who knows? Maybe you'll want to start your own business someday or hire on as an apprentice somewhere. But—just—make sure you stick around. Or, if you leave, don't go too far."

"Cottleson's is like home to me," I said softly. "I don't think I'd ever go too far."

Two days later, Phillip was back at the tavern with a very official-looking document that asserted his claim to part-ownership of the tavern.

"If we settle this now, if you pay me half the value of the property, I'll be content with that," Phillip told Leona. "If you fight me on it, I'll take you to a court of law and sue you for the whole thing. I'll win, too. That's what Barney says. Better off for you to sell the place and give me half the money, or you'll lose everything."

Sallie and I eavesdropped on their whole conversation, which took place in the kitchen one autumn morning. As soon as he left, we rushed in to commiserate. Leona sat at the table as she had that one night, her head in her hands, her whole body dejected.

"I don't know what to do," she wailed, as Sallie bent over to give her a hug and I started a kettle of water for tea. "Should I take out a loan for the money he wants? But then what if business goes soft again and I can't pay the loan back? But I can't sell Cottleson's—I can't. But if I refuse to sell and I lose everything—"

"To me, Phillip seems like the kind of man who will never be satisfied," Sallie said, pulling up a chair next to Leona's stool. "If you take out a loan but you still own the tavern, sooner or later he'll come back with another scheme. As long as you own this property, he'll think half of it belongs to him, no matter what you pay him."

"But then—but then—if I sell the tavern—"

I poured everyone a mug of steaming liquid. "I think you first need to find out if his document is valid," I said. "Hire a lawyer now that you can afford one."

Leona halfheartedly sipped her tea. "I suppose. But I don't even know any lawyers. How can I find one who's trustworthy?"

I settled across from the two women and blew on my tea. "I wonder if Raymond would take your case," I said.

Leona and Sallie stared at me. "Raymond Lemkey?" Leona repeated. "The one who argues cases for the queen?"

"Is that what he's doing now?"

"You know *him*?" Sallie demanded.

"Well, I used to. When I lived in Thrush Hollow, he—"

"You know, I'm finding it very hard to believe that so much was transpiring in Thrush Hollow during the time you lived there," Leona interrupted. "I grew up in Tambleham and Lowford and a lot of places that were larger than Thrush Hollow, and *nothing* exciting ever happened in any of them. Whereas you live in the smallest town in a dull corner of the kingdom, and you meet Safe-Keepers and Dream-Makers and famous attorneys and—and—I don't know *who* you might produce next!"

I grinned. "I think that's it for my impressive connections," I said. "And I don't know if Raymond would be interested in the case. But I'll ask him."

"Yes, Kellen," Leona replied in a strangled voice. "Why don't you do that?"

Raymond, in fact, was delighted to take Leona's case. I visited him in his law office, where two haughty clerks made me wait for nearly an hour before they took my name in to him. I was gratified at the alacrity with which they hurried back out to tell me the senior partner would see me right away, and how very sorry they were that they had kept me waiting.

"Kellen, my dear!" Raymond greeted me in his expansive way. I had time to notice that his white hair was elegantly styled and his clothes were extremely fine before I realized that he was looking me over with critical attention. "The face I recognize, and of course the name, but I do not recall you dressing in such unconventional clothing during the time I knew you in Thrush Hollow," he said. "What has changed?"

"I came to Wodenderry alone and unsure of myself, and I thought it might be better to dress as a boy," I said.

"And has it been?"

"I think life went easier for me when I first arrived. But I think I could assume my true identity now and not suffer for it," I admitted.

"Then why don't you?"

I thought of Leona and Sallie, and how astonished they would be. Just the other day Leona had claimed I was like a nephew to her. How would she feel if I suddenly turned into a niece? I thought of Gryffin, and how it might look to everyone if it was known he had singled out some nameless woman for his attention. He was the most-watched man in the kingdom. Would people not pressure him to explain his intentions?

"It still seems easier," I said. "So don't betray me."

He made a broad gesture with his hand. "Betray you! Never. Not even accidentally. I never make such crass mistakes."

Indeed, he came to Cottleson's that very night and met with Leona in the kitchen, where, of course, I was preparing the evening meal. He referred to me incessantly as "Kellen, my boy," and lost no chance to tell Leona what a fine young man I was. It was all I could do to keep from having a fit of the giggles.

But he took the case, which was what really mattered. "Let me see the document that this fine fellow Barney has crafted," Raymond demanded. "Let me see, let me see . . . ah. Indeed. Hmm. Well, he has some knowledge of the law, but not enough to circumvent me. This might take a little time, a few weeks, a few months at most, but we shall prevail, my good young woman. Don't you despair."

Leona seemed pleased but bemused when he finally left, Barney's file in hand. "What an odd man," she said. "He makes me feel as if I have just been blown about by a windstorm. And yet I like him."

"He'll help you," I promised.

She laughed. "Just when I think I really know you, Kellen, you come up with another surprise."

"Not any more," I said. "All my surprises are done with."

Well, of course, I had one more secret that might astonish her, but I did not propose to share that just yet. I was perfectly happy in my new life, in my assumed role; I had no immediate plans to change.

"You say that," she replied. "But I have a feeling that I will be even more startled at whoever you produce next."

After the first three months of Gryffin's patronage, business slacked off a little at Cottleson's—not enough to hurt Leona's finances, but enough to enable us to catch a breath from time to time or enjoy a slow hour once in a while. Gryffin still made semi-regular appearances, both in public and in private; the weeks he could not find time to visit the tavern, I went to the palace to have breakfast with him. He offered to introduce me to Queen Lirabel, or the handsome prince and his charming wife, but I was too shy. And too strange. If I was going to encounter royalty, I wanted to be beautifully dressed in a gown that enabled me to make a formal curtsy. So I would not let him take me to the public areas of the palace, but we often sat in the royal gardens, until the weather started to grow too cold. Then we sat in the conservatory, which was just as green, and happily passed the hours.

Raymond came by the tavern now and then to assure Leona that he was working on her case. "I've been retracing your parents' journey through life," he told her once. "Visiting all the towns where they once lived, to make sure they did not file any wills that might serve as counterclaims. Quite the nomads they were!"

"Yes," said Leona. "I think that might be why I am so attached to the tavern. After we built it, we finally stayed in one place for longer than a year. I was so tired of traveling. I wanted a permanent home."

"Well," said Raymond, "I'll make sure you have one."

It was perhaps six weeks before Wintermoon when another one of my old friends showed up at Cottleson's, and everything changed again.

Chapter Twenty-Two

It was late afternoon, and I was cleaning the kitchen and beginning to consider dinner, when Leona came in from the taproom. She looked flustered and a little befuddled, and once she was through the swinging door she stopped and leaned against the wall.

"Oh, my," she said in a faint voice.

I gave her an inquiring look. "What's wrong?"

"There is—a man just walked in and he is—I swear, Kellen, he is the most attractive man I have ever seen." She straightened up and began fooling with her auburn hair, pulling it down from its habitual bun, then rewinding it and pinning it back in place. "I couldn't even *speak* to him. I went to ask him if he wanted dinner, or beer or wine—and I said *weer* or *bine*! A glass of bine! What an idiot! I can't go back out there."

I was laughing. "Well, do you want me to take his order?"

"Yes. And tell him I'm—tell him I'm—well, don't mention me. Maybe he didn't even notice."

I dried my hands and smoothed down my vest and headed out to the taproom. The new arrival was sitting in one of the side booths, studying his menu intently. "Afternoon, sir, could I take your order?" I asked. But when he looked up at me, I was almost as dumbfounded as Leona. Handsome, yes, with a fair head of curls and melting brown eyes. But it was not just his good looks that had me gaping. "Chase? Chase Beerin?"

His face grave, he scanned me. "Yes, that's my name. But I don't—wait, you do look familiar, but I—"

"Kellen Carmichael," I said helpfully. "You stayed at my mother's house in Thrush Hollow—oh, three years ago. You went with me to see my friend Gryffin to take a look at his legs—"

Now his expression changed, his whole face lightening as he smiled. "Kellen! Of course I remember! I have thought of you often since that day—you and your friend both. What are you doing in Wodenderry?" He glanced at my attire. "Still dressed as a boy, I see."

I slid into the booth on the opposite bench. We were usually too busy to fraternize with customers, but there were only a couple of other diners in place at the moment, and Chase was special. "Oh, the costume seemed easier to keep when I came to Wodenderry," I said dismissively. "But no one here knows the truth! So don't let on."

"All right," he said, amused. "But what brought you to the city? And how is Gryffin? Still suffering or much improved?"

"You don't know?" I demanded. "You haven't figured it out?"

"I suppose not, since I have no idea what you mean."

"Gryffin! He's the Dream-Maker! He came to Woden-derry a year ago and now lives in the palace with the queen!"

Chase collapsed back against the booth, clearly aston-ished. "No! I realized that the Dream-Maker was a young man with limited use of his legs, but I—what a marvelous thing! I am so pleased for him." Then he sat up straighter and frowned a little. "Although—haven't I heard that the Dream-Maker is confined to a wheeled chair? Is he worse, then? For when I saw him, I thought he showed some prom-ise of significant improvement."

"He had a setback," I said carefully. "His legs were injured. Again. The pain is severe enough these days that it keeps him from even trying to walk very much."

"That's a shame," Chase said. "Has he seen a practitioner?"

"I think the royal physician treats him."

From the expression on Chase's face I gathered the impression that he did not think so highly of the queen's medical man. But all he said was, "I am sorry to hear of his condition."

"But tell me about you!" I exclaimed. "You came to the royal city to study medicine, you said. Have you been suc-cessful?"

He nodded. "Yes, I am almost through with my studies, and I have been seeing patients for the past six months. I love the work, Kellen. I feel like I have found my calling. But I'm so busy! I can't remember the last night I went out for a night of fun with my friends. In fact, today I sat in my office and realized that I practically *have* no friends, and if I didn't make some effort to retain the one or two fellows who still speak to me, I would soon have none at all."

I thought of Leona, blushing in the kitchen. "So I don't suppose you've had time to get married," I said offhandedly.

He laughed. "No! But now that I know Gryffin is the Dream-Maker, I will presume on past friendship and go seek him out. And that's exactly what I'll ask for. *Dream-Maker, I'll say, can you find me a wife?*"

At that exact moment, Leona stepped back into the tap-room, carrying a tray. She had a studiedly casual expression on her face, and she crossed the room with a rather stately step that I knew was intended to cover her slight trembling. "I see one of your friends has joined you," she said to Chase. She hadn't looked at me, because she couldn't take her eyes off the handsome doctor. "I brought a selection of bread and beer for you to enjoy while you peruse the menu."

"Thank you," Chase said in his earnest way. "You are most kind."

Now she did look my way, and she almost dropped the tray when she saw who was sitting there. "Kellen! What are you doing? Why are you—" She glanced from me to Chase and back to me.

I jumped up. My smile was so wide I thought my whole face must have disappeared behind it. "Leona. Let me introduce you to Chase Beerin. He did a kindness for a friend of mine once, and I have always wanted a chance to repay the favor. Won't you sit here and talk to him until his friends arrive? I'll go make him a special dinner."

I was no Dream-Maker, of course, and I would not have called myself a matchmaker, either, but it was obvious by the end of that first dinner that Chase found Leona as delightful as she found him. He stayed at the tavern long after his friends left, and Leona snatched maybe a dozen free moments during the course of the evening to pause at his table and exchange a few more words. Every time Sallie came into the kitchen she gave me a significant look, and I made more than my usual number of trips out into the taproom to check on the situation for myself. Chase stayed through the cleanup process, even helping us carry dirty plates and glasses into the kitchen. He and Leona were once again sitting in the booth, talking, when I finally went to bed.

He was back the next evening. And the next. He missed two nights, but was back at the tavern for the next three. Pretty soon we began to expect him to be present four days out of five, and Leona stopped looking so nervous when he first stepped through the door. The smile on her face remained, however.

Oddly, it was several weeks before Gryffin and Chase were at Cottleson's on the same evening. Of course, I had told Gryffin the very next day about our old friend suddenly returned to our lives.

"Chase Beerin. I remember him as the kindest man I've ever met," Gryffin said. We were having breakfast in the royal conservatory, where the windows were steamy with heat. Outside, it was damp and chilly.

"Yes, and I don't think he's changed," I replied. "I'm

hoping he and Leona will fall in love! They seem very interested in each other, and he's at the tavern almost every night, but I can't be sure the story will go as I want it to." I folded my hands before me in a supplicant's clasp. "Please, Dream-Maker, make this wish come true."

He waved his hands grandly. "Poof! It is so." Then he gave me a rather stern look. "How many times do I need to tell you not to waste dreams on other people? You're supposed to offer your own hopes to the Dream-Maker."

I scooped up another piece of fruit. Imported during this season and very expensive. "Why can't I make wishes for my friends if I want to?" I said. "I think half the wishes I've ever spoken in my life have been for other people."

"Because what if you're wrong about what they desire?" he replied. "You think they want to travel to Wodenderry to see the queen, when all they really want is to stay home with their familiar circle of friends."

I ate a bite of pastry and thought this over. "Did you wish for me to come to Wodenderry?" I said at last. "And did you think I might have come against my will?"

"I'm the Dream-Maker," he said. "I can't make my own dreams come true."

"That doesn't seem fair," I said. "And it also doesn't answer my question."

He shrugged a little, and then he smiled. "I wanted you to come here so much," he said. "But it was so long before you arrived. And then I found you had been here for weeks without telling me. And you're still not here as yourself. You're dressed as a boy—you're in deep disguise. And I wonder if all these things, taken together, mean you didn't really want to come. And if they mean you wish you weren't here."

His hand lay on the table between us. I covered it with my own. "Gryffin. Of all the things you might need to worry about, that's the one thing you can cast aside. I'm in Wodenderry because you're here and because I want to be where you are. I'm in disguise because I thought it would be easier to move into my new life this way."

"But you're in your new life," he said. "Time to be yourself."

I laughed a little. "But what will I say to Leona? And Sallie? What will they think of me when I reveal who I am?"

"We all have to do that at some point," he said. "We all have to reveal our true natures to the people we've come to trust. A disguise is all very well in a cold and hostile world, but when you come to a place of warmth and safety, you have to risk being yourself."

"I know. Maybe. You're right, but I—I don't know that I'm ready yet. Leona trusts me so much! I don't know if I want to see her face when she realizes I've lied to her."

His fingers tightened over mine. "I wish you would," he said, his voice very close to a whisper. "I want everyone to see you for who you are."

So that was unsettling, but in a somewhat thrilling way. I spent the next two days trying to decide how to tell Leona, what exactly to confess. *I know you thought we were close as kin. I know I told you I had no more surprises. . . .* It was hard to find the words to explain such a deception, no matter how necessary the trick had seemed when it was first embraced.

Luckily for me, bigger events were unfolding. It was easy to set aside the need for my own confession.

As Wintermoon grew even closer, Phillip started to haunt the tavern, arriving at odd hours—very early or very late—sometimes not entirely sober. I gathered that whatever venture he wanted the money for would be set in motion upon the new year, and so he was starting to grow desperate for funds. More than once, I saw shadowy figures lurking just outside the back door—Barney, I assumed, and some of his confederates—as Phillip came in to wheedle and threaten Leona. More than once, Chase and a couple of his friends offered to throw him out in the street, though Phillip usually backed off before it came to violence.

"Maybe I should just do it," Leona said tiredly one day after Chase had kicked Phillip out again. "Maybe I should just sell the tavern."

A chorus of "no"s came from Sallie and Chase and me—and a new voice, raised at the front door. "No," the voice repeated, and we all spun around to see Raymond Lemkey taking a pose at the threshold. He looked very dapper, in fine clothes and a top hat, and his shoulders were covered with a glittering dust of snow. "No, I don't believe it will come to that," Raymond said, stepping inside with a hint of a swagger. "Leona, you might want to invite your brother back in. I have news for you both."

"I'll get him," Chase said, and pushed his way out the door.

It was mid-afternoon on a cold, snowy day, and there were very few patrons on hand. Most of them were long-standing customers who had some interest in the outcome of this struggle, so Leona didn't mind if they stayed as Phillip came snarling back in, Chase at his heels.

"So? What is it? You've found a way to settle my claim?" Phillip demanded.

"Sit, sit, sit," Raymond said, and soon we had all disposed ourselves around one of the center tables. Sallie and I had pulled up seats alongside everyone else, since we figured the outcome of the lawsuit would affect us almost as much as Leona.

Raymond pulled a pair of spectacles out of his pocket and unfolded a piece of paper with many elaborate flourishes. "In my role as legal counsel to Leona Cottleson, I have carefully examined the few documents left behind by Eric and Nettie Cottleson," he began in a very formal style. "Birth records, marriage records, rental leases at properties in towns throughout the kingdom, purchase agreements for this tavern, that sort of thing. I have investigated in every town where they once had residence. There was no formal will."

"Right," Phillip said, hitching his chair closer. "And Barney says that when a will is missing, the heirs get to split the property in two. That's what Barney says."

"Indeed, and Barney is most well informed. Yet there is a little-known provision of the royal code—in effect in Wodenderry for two hundred years, ever since Queen Lirabel's great-great-grandfather signed it into law—that pertains to situations like this. It is called the 'intent by action' statute by which we may infer that one conveys through one's activities exactly what one plans to do."

We all stared at him a moment. "What?" Leona said faintly.

Raymond waved a hand. I caught a glimpse of a lace cuff beneath his jacket sleeve. "Your *actions*, Leona, have been to work diligently in the tavern since your father's death, demonstrating your intent to make it a profitable and prosperous business. Phillip's *actions* have been to show no care or interest in the business at all, demonstrating his intent to live a life unburdened by responsibility. Going by this measure, Leona has proved her claim to the property and Phillip has not. The tavern is yours, free and clear."

All of us exclaimed in pleasure—except Phillip, who slammed an open hand down on the table. "I don't believe you!" Phillip shouted. "I want my day in court!"

Raymond nodded. "And you shall have it, if you like. I will argue your sister's claim. You—or perhaps one of your estimable friends—can argue yours." He adjusted a cuff link, then glanced up to give Phillip a piercing look. "I suppose you know I have not lost a case in the past year. And I have argued dozens."

Phillip pounded a fist down, then jumped to his feet and took three rough strides around the room. I saw Chase watching him, ready to take him on in a fight if the young man turned ugly. But most of my attention was on Phillip, whose headlong motion came to a sputtering stop as he halted in the middle of the room and stared back at all of us.

His face had changed so rapidly from anger to despair that, for the first time, I actually felt sorry for him.

"It's not fair," he said, his voice low and a little shaky. I remembered again that he was really only a boy—my own age, or thereabouts. "I'm to get nothing? He was my father, too."

Leona came to her feet, though Chase caught at her arm as if to keep her from going to her brother. "You have a home here anytime you want," she said steadily. "And a job, if you want to work. I would never turn you out of the tavern. But I won't give it up for you. I won't let you take it from me. I'll share it, if you like."

"No!" he shouted, and he balled up his hands at his sides. "I want—what I want—I don't want *this*. I want to take my inheritance and turn it into something else."

"Not a bad idea, but you don't have an inheritance," Raymond said. "Your sister's offer is a good one. If you work beside her for three years, putting in the same kind of hours she does, the 'intent by action' statute will apply to you as well. At that point the court might have to reconsider—"

"But I don't want to work here! I want—you don't under-stand what I want!" he cried, and his voice was so pitiful that I continued to feel sorry for him, even though he was behaving so abominably. "To be stuck here—trapped in Wodenderry—I have other places to go, things *I* want to do! I can't—it would be death to me, staying at this place all the time."

"Well, then," Raymond said, "this place will never be yours."

Phillip stared at him for a moment, stared at Leona, then flung himself out the front door without another word.

A smattering of applause came from the other patrons of the tavern, as well as a few calls of, "That's the way, Leona!" and "Good job! Congratulations!" The rest of us sat there a few more moments, a little stunned.

"Well," Leona said finally. "That was certainly dramatic. I'm so relieved that I'm a little numb! Raymond, how can I ever thank you?" She laughed. "Besides paying your bill, I mean."

Raymond adjusted the set of his suit jacket. "I think, one of Kellen's admirable dinners will be all the additional thanks I require," he said. "And perhaps, now and then, if you have a friend who needs legal advice, you might mention my name."

"That I will certainly do," Leona replied.

I hurried into the kitchen to make Raymond's meal—and, indeed, begin preparations for all the other dinners I would be serving that night. I was completely delighted for Leona, of course, and yet I found myself feeling a great deal of sympathy for the thwarted and disappointed Phillip. He was rather a wretched boy, but then, I had never seen him engaged in any enterprise that interested him. Tavern-keeping certainly did not, and why should it? He had his own dreams to pursue; he did not need to be tied to his father's. I found myself wishing that Gryffin had been present during one of the moments Phillip had dropped by the tavern to make another of his threats. Maybe the alchemy of the Dream-Maker's magic would have turned his ill-natured demands into impossibly delicate dreams. Maybe Gryffin would have known how to make even Phillip's desires come true.

Chapter Twenty-Three

he day before Wintermoon, a package arrived from my mother. I had sent her an inexpensive Wintermoon gift—and one for Georgie, as well—and I expected the rather small box to contain something as slight and frivolous as the lace collar I had mailed to her. Indeed, there was nothing very special about the gloves she had enclosed, though she had knitted them herself, but the letter that accompanied them almost made me faint to the kitchen floor.

Dearest Kellen:

I have got sad news to report today. Your father has died. It seems he has been alive all this time, even though I haven't heard a word from him for at least two years. He settled in Merendon and started a store, still a peddler but not traveling about so much, I suppose. Anyway, it seems that the store was very successful, and when he knew he was dying, he sold it to a friend for a lot of money. Half of it goes to me and half to you—or, as he says, "my only living child," so at least we know he never married again and started another family. You must come to Thrush Hollow to get it, but it is more than five hundred pieces in gold for each of us. I know! Who ever thought we would see so much money? I have already bought Georgie some new clothes, and I am going to get him a puppy. I hope your Wintermoon is a very happy one.

 Love,

 your mother

I was reading the letter through for the third time when I felt someone touch my arm. "Kellen?" It was Leona. "Kellen? Are you sick? You've turned so pale. Should I go fetch Chase? He's in the other room."

I looked at her, my eyes so wide I thought I should be able to see the whole world at once. "Leona," I said. "My father died and left me a lot of money."

"He did? I didn't even know your father was still alive. I'm sorry, of course—"

"No, he left me *five hundred gold pieces*! I haven't seen him since I was nine years old! I thought he was dead! I can't believe this!"

Now she clapped her hands together. "Kellen, that's wonderful! You can—you can buy a house for that! You can open up a business or travel the country or—I don't even know what anyone would do with so much money! When do you get it?"

"I have to go to Thrush Hollow, my mother says. I have to sign some documents, I suppose."

Her face was mischievous. "Take Raymond with you if there are documents involved. Or *any* kind of inheritance."

"I don't think I'll need Raymond. This should be very straightforward. I'll just—I'll just—I think I'll just sit down a moment."

Leona ran to get Sallie and Chase, to tell them the news, and soon the three of them were crowding around me, full of congratulations and contagious joy.

"You won't have to work for a living anymore, that's for sure," Sallie said.

"I was just thinking that, and I can't bear it!" Leona exclaimed. "Kellen, you promised me you would never move away. Even if you become as wealthy as the queen, you'll have to stay right here in the city. You'll buy a house down the street. You'll come over every morning to have tea, and you'll be my cook on the days I need an extra hand."

"Well, I'll work through Wintermoon, at least," I said, still feeling dazed. "I don't want to travel over the holiday. Then I guess I'll go to Thrush Hollow."

"You *guess* you'll go? You *guess*?" Sallie derided. "If I had that much gold waiting for me, I'd be on the stagecoach tomorrow."

We were still babbling in the kitchen, ignoring all our customers, when the door swung open and Gryffin rolled in. "Here you are!" he said. "I was beginning to think you'd all fallen into a snowdrift somewhere."

"Gryffin!" I exclaimed. "You'll never guess—my mother writes to say I've inherited a fortune from my father."

"Really? That's wonderful! What will you do with it?"

I laughed. "I have no idea!"

Sallie was beaming. "That's what it means to be best friends with a Dream-Maker," she said, nodding at me. "Your every wish is granted."

"I used to wish that my father would do something to prove he loved me, and now I suppose he has," I said. "But I never thought to wish for *money*!"

"Then maybe your wish got mixed up with mine," Sallie said, holding her hand out. "So I'll take that gold now, thank you very much."

We all laughed some more, and probably would have remained there another hour, talking like idiots, if there hadn't been a crash of glass from the other room. Leona started. "Oh! There are twenty people waiting to be served!" she cried, heading for the door. "Sallie, come help! I don't think Kellen's going to be much use to us today."

"I will be!" I called after them. "Just give me a minute and I'll get dinner started."

I turned back to Gryffin, to find him shaking hands with Chase Beerin. "You look just as I remember," Gryffin said. "I have always wished I had a chance to thank you for everything you did for me that day. I had forgotten what it was like to be out of pain."

Chase squatted down by Gryffin's chair, his face professional and serious. "Yes, but it seems like you have remembered pain now," he replied. "Kellen says you were injured and never really recovered. Could I take a look at your legs? Perhaps there is something I could do to help you."

Gryffin looked uncertain, but he covered the expression

with a smile. "Oh, I'm sure you didn't come here tonight planning on physicking the customers."

"I don't mind. I'm rather interested in your case."

"You can go to my room for some privacy," I said. I pointed at the door that led to my small chamber and hoped I had remembered to make up the bed that morning.

"Thank you," Chase said, and motioned Gryffin forward. I saw Gryffin hesitate a moment, giving me an unreadable look, and then he set his wheels in motion. Chase followed him into my room and shut the door.

I began the preparations for dinner, but my mind was far from the bacon and the flour and the parsley. Would Chase really be able to offer Gryffin some relief from his incessant pain? If so, why had Gryffin looked so uneasy at the thought? What was transpiring behind the door of that small room?

I set a pan in the oven to bake and mixed up fresh ingredients for a dinner cake. Then I washed my hands and crossed to my room and gave a soft knock. Gryffin's muffled voice bid me to come in.

The scene was strangely reminiscent of the first night we had met Chase—the three of us gathered in a small room lit by candles, Gryffin stretched out on the bed with his legs uncovered, somber expressions all around. But Chase's face looked hopeful, I thought.

"What have you discovered?" I demanded, sitting on the bed next to Gryffin, so close our shoulders were almost touching.

"I can't be sure of anything until I do a more thorough examination," Chase replied. "But I think I could do him some good. It would require a surgical operation to repair some of the damage to the bones. And then it would require that Gryffin learn how to walk again, and practice new exercises every day. I don't think he will ever be entirely out of pain, or ever walk without the use of a cane, but I believe I could restore some mobility and relieve at least the worst of the agony. I don't think I can heal him, but I can make him better."

I clapped my hands together. "Oh, Gryffin! What wonderful news!"

The smile on Chase's face was a little sad. "Gryffin does not seem convinced of that," he said.

I felt myself grow tense. "Why? Is he afraid of the surgery? Gryffin, it can hardly be worse than what you live through every day."

"Well, yes, it can," Chase said candidly. "It can be quite gloriously painful. But a surgical incision will improve, whereas his current condition will not."

I pulled back enough so I could view Gryffin's face. He had flung one of my blankets over his legs, but I had seen them when I first came in—still the twisted, thin, bruised-looking sticks they had always been. "I don't understand," I said quietly. "Why are you afraid?"

Gryffin looked from me to Chase, his face a study in vulnerability. "I want to do it, truly I do," he said. "For myself? I would love to be so strong I could put aside this wheeled chair and walk across the kingdom. But what if—what if I only have my magic because of my pain? What if I lose the Dream-Maker's power? I have done so much good for so many people. Wouldn't it be selfish to pursue my own happiness and leave everyone else with no hope of achieving theirs?"

"Oh, Gryffin," I whispered, and put both my arms around him. I could feel my tears start, and I rested my cheek against his shoulder so he wouldn't see. "That wouldn't be selfish at all."

The small smile was back on Chase's face. "If pain is what anchors the magic to you, I don't know that you would need to worry," the doctor answered. "As I said, I don't think you'll ever be free of it. Just much improved."

"Yes, but then, perhaps the magic is diluted as much as the pain is. . . ."

I lifted my head. "Then perhaps it will be someone else's turn to be Dream-Maker," I said rather fiercely. "As the power passed from Melinda to you, so it will pass from you to someone else."

"But what if it doesn't?" Gryffin said.

Chase shrugged. "If it doesn't? Then people must work harder to achieve their own desires," he said. "Besides, I've often wondered. Is there really only one Dream-Maker at a time? I've witnessed things—moments of bravery, acts of mercy—that lead me to think all of us can make dreams come true for someone else, at least once or twice in our lives. I've done it, I know I have. I've seen others do it as well. Why shouldn't that be a charge on all of us? Each of us be Dream-Makers when we can. Why should all that power reside in the hands of one hurt boy?"

I gave a watery chuckle, my face still pressed against Gryffin's bony shoulder. "That sounds like heresy," I said.

Chase shrugged. "Well, I have always been the kind of

man to ask questions," he said. "No reason to stop asking them now." He came to his feet, and both of us looked up at him. "Think about it," he urged as he reached for the door. "Discuss it with Kellen. I am here most nights. You can find me again when you want to talk."

"Can you check on the oven on your way through the kitchen?" I asked. He laughed, assented, and left the room, closing the door behind him.

Gryffin and I sat in silence for some moments. My arms were still around him, and one of his hands had come up to hook itself over my wrist.

"What are you thinking?" I asked at last.

"I don't know what to think," he replied. "I am afraid to do it, and I am afraid not to. It is not something I ever let myself hope for before. It is not something I ever wished for. How can a dream come true if it wasn't even your dream?"

"I wished it for you," I said. "It would be my dream come true if you were whole and out of pain."

The softest of laughs, almost a sigh. "I told you before not to waste your dreams on other people."

I lifted my head. "What are you telling me? That you *don't* want to be well? That you *don't* want to be able to walk again?"

"I don't want to lose the power," he admitted. "Not just because I am afraid to see magic go out of the world. But because—because—who will I be then? What will I be if I am no longer Dream-Maker?"

I dropped my arms, though I wanted to grab his shoulders and shake him. "Who were you *before* you were

Dream-Maker?" I demanded. "You were the smartest boy I'd ever met. You worked harder than anyone I knew. You set goals for yourself that would have seemed impossible for anyone else, but I knew you would achieve them. You wanted to come to Wodenderry and study—well, here you are in Wodenderry. If the power leaves you, then follow that old desire. Become a lawyer, like Raymond, or a doctor, like Chase. How many dreams could you make come true then?" I put my hands on either side of his face. "If the magic leaves you, you will be who you always were," I whispered. "You will be the person who matters most to me in the world."

His hands covered mine where they lay against his cheeks. "Would you love me if I wasn't Dream-Maker?" he asked in the smallest voice.

I replied, in tones as soft as his own, "I will love you no matter what."

The next day was Wintermoon, the most magical day of the year. Time to look ahead to the future and refine your hopes and dreams. Time to tie your wishes to a Wintermoon wreath and watch them get written in flame against a moonlit sky. Wishes had been generally in flux lately, I thought, at least for the people I was closest to. It would be hard to know exactly what items to attach to the great rope of greenery hanging over the bar at Cottleson's. It would be hard to brace for the new year, since it seemed so much had already happened—and so much was still undecided.

Leona said much the same thing that morning as we did a final sweep of the taproom before opening for lunch.

"What do I have left to wish for?" she said. "I've secured the tavern. Business has been wonderful. I've fallen in love. My friends have discovered riches. I think it would only be greedy for me to ask for anything more."

"Well, I've still got plenty left to want," Sallie said, bustling up with her hands full of ribbons. "I'm going to ask for love and money and fame and anything else I can think of."

What I wanted was a way to make a graceful transition, from who I was now to who I wanted to be. To change, as Gryffin had asked, from a boy back into a girl. Partly because he had asked—but only partly. I loved him, and I had said so, and I wanted to be able to show the world that I did. And I wanted to be myself as I did so.

In the end, I took out the carved coral disk that the itinerant peddler had given me so long ago, the one he had said represented femininity. I had brought it with me from Thrush Hollow but hidden it in the very bottom drawer of my dresser, not wanting to be troubled by any of its ancient magic. But now, at Wintermoon, on the cusp of a new year, I thought it might help me cross a threshold from pretend to real. I attached it to the wreath and silently spoke my wish.

But, like Sallie, I had many other things to hope for. Ever since Melinda had made that memorable visit to Thrush Hollow, I had collected a scattering of wishes, and when I couldn't bring them to the Dream-Maker, I had attached them to Wintermoon wreaths. Today, I breathed wishes for each of the people I knew and cared about, specific ones when I guessed what they were, and general ones when I didn't. I asked for Gryffin to be well and out of pain. I asked for Sallie to find love and happiness, for Leona's great good fortune to continue. I spared a thought for Phillip, whom we had not seen since Raymond's announcement, and I wished him a little good fortune of his own. I remembered Sarah and Bo, Emily and Randal, my mother and Georgie. After I had run through the names of all the people I knew, I ended the way I always did: *Let everyone have at least one wish come true.* And then I tied a knot of multicolored ribbons to the greenery, a rainbow spiral of undifferentiated desire, and let each one represent what it would, so long as it was good.

"We'll burn that tonight," Leona said, coming up behind me. "Chase's coming with some of his friends. Will Gryffin be here?"

"He said he would," I replied.

"What has he decided about the surgery?"

"I don't know that he has decided yet. But I hope he'll do it."

Just then the door opened to admit our first customer of the day. But this was a familiar one. "Ayler!" Leona exclaimed. "In town for Wintermoon?"

The Safe-Keeper gave each of us a warm hug and his dreamy smile. "Just for a few days," he said. "But I thought I'd spend the holiday here. I assume you're burning a wreath tonight?"

"Yes, and it will be quite the occasion," Leona said gaily. "Even the Dream-Maker will be here. Don't you think that means our wishes stand an even better chance of coming true?"

"Indeed, I do," Ayler replied. "I can hardly wait to see what the new year brings."

"After this year? Neither can I," Leona said with a laugh.

What the next hour brought was a steady stream of customers, all of them hoping, no doubt, to catch a glimpse of the Dream-Maker on this particular day. Foreseeing this possibility, we had pressed Sallie's sisters into service again, and I divided my time between working in the kitchen and waiting on tables in the taproom.

It was mid-afternoon when I approached one of the booths where two women were seated. Assessing them automatically as I got closer, I assumed that their fair hair and matching profiles indicated that they were probably sisters. But when I arrived smiling at the table, and they both looked up from their menus at the same time, I realized they were twins. Their features were so similar they could have been one person set before a mirror, except that the one woman was smiling and the other was not.

"Good afternoon," I said. "I'm Kellen. What can I get you today?"

"The roasted chicken sounds very good to me," said the smiling woman.

Leona came hurrying up beside me. "We might be out of the roasted chicken," she apologized. "It's been a more popular item than we anticipated. But the braised turkey is quite tasty."

"Then perhaps I'll try the turkey," the woman replied.

Her sister was watching me with a frown on her face. "Why are you dressed like that?" she asked abruptly.

Leona, who had turned away, turned back in surprise. I felt a blush come to my face, but I maintained a nonchalant expression. "Dressed like what?" I said.

The frowning twin waved her hand at my clothes. "Like that. Like a boy. You're a young woman under that shapeless vest and those baggy trousers."

"Eleda," her sister said in an admonitory voice. "Perhaps that's a secret."

"Well, it's a ridiculous secret," Eleda said roundly. "No reason to be pretending anymore."

The smiling twin sent an apologetic look my way. "My sister is a Truth-Teller," she explained. "It's sometimes most inconvenient. I'm sorry if her plain-speaking makes your life more difficult."

I couldn't respond. I risked one quick look at Leona, who was staring at me in complete confusion, and then I dropped my gaze to the floor. "It was a secret that had to come out sometime," I mumbled.

Eleda made an impatient noise. "Maybe that's why Gryffin wanted us to come over here today," she said. "*I* thought it was because he wanted us to try some fine cooking, but maybe he wanted us to be proclaiming truths."

"You, not us," her sister replied with a merry laugh. "And the truth is, I'd like to try some of that turkey."

"Right away," I whispered, and ran for the kitchen.

There I stood for a moment, my back braced against the wall, my heart racing, my blood tingling through every vein. *Had* Gryffin sent a Truth-Teller to Cottleson's to expose me? He knew dozens of Safe-Keepers and Truth-Tellers, for many of them consulted regularly with the queen—and he had been very clear on this topic not long ago. If he had had a wish of his own, it was to see me take my true identity. He would never betray me himself, but might he send a Truth-Teller to the place where I lived, on the chance that the secret was ready to be told? Yes, I thought, he would. And it seemed he had been right. For the truth had come out; my secret had been revealed. My Wintermoon wish was set to come true even before the burning of the wreath.

Sallie's sister glanced over at me from where she sat, rolling out bread. "What's wrong with you? See a spider in the salad?" she asked.

I shook my head. "No—I think I saw a ghost of myself walking through the tavern door."

"You saw *what*?"

"Never mind. Would you take a shift waiting tables? I'll stay in the kitchen and cook."

So I didn't have to face the sharp-eyed Truth-Teller again—and I took care not to be alone with Leona for the rest of the day. By the time the early dark of winter fell, the tavern had completely cleared out, as all the customers hurried home to their friends and families. Sallie came into the kitchen to collect her siblings.

"Time to go home," she said, pulling on her coat. "Our father's probably already got the bonfire started."

"Is everyone gone out front?" I asked.

"Everyone except Ayler," Sallie said. "Leona asked if you could bring out a pot of tea for the two of them. She's sitting in the back booth talking with him."

I nodded. The reckoning had arrived.

Chapter Twenty-four

made up a tray of tea and leftover turkey, with a little bread on the side, and I added enough plates to serve three. Then I carried it out to a dim booth in the back of the tavern, laid out the places and the food, and slid onto the bench next to Ayler.

"Warm Wintermoon to you both," I said in a subdued voice.

Ayler glanced over at me, a smile on his dreamy face. "Leona tells me your secret has been discovered."

I nodded. I was watching Leona. She was leaning against the back of the booth, her auburn hair a bright color in the dim light. She was not smiling, but she did not seem to be angry. "I suppose I should say I'm sorry I lied to you," I said straight out. "And I am. I was not so much concealing secrets from *you* as concealing myself from the world. I did not know what to expect when I came to Wodenderry. By the time I realized I could safely be myself with you, the lie had already been told. I was not sure how to then present the truth."

She nodded. "I understand that, Kellen, I truly do. But how much I wish you had trusted me! I would never have turned you away, no matter who you were or what strange tale you had to tell."

"I hoped so," I said. "I am very glad to hear that it's true."

"And I know I should be angry, but somehow I'm not," she said. "In fact, mostly I'm amazed at how you could maintain such a deception! If I suddenly took the notion to dress as a man, I would be tripped up a dozen times a day. I would forget how to speak or how to walk or even how to refer to myself, but you never made those mistakes."

I laughed a little. "I have been practicing for this role for much of my life, I suppose," I said. "You told me once that your mother wasn't interested in her daughter after her son was born. It was much the same in my household, but worse. My mother wanted a boy so badly she pretended that's what I was. She dressed me as a boy—she treated me as one. Not until I was fourteen did I wear skirts or style my hair. I'm more used to a boy's mannerisms than a girl's."

Now Leona looked shocked. "Kellen, I'm so sorry. That's dreadful."

I shrugged. "I have learned some useful lessons, and I like the freedom that I've been granted," I said. "It has not been so bad."

Ayler stirred and spoke. "But isn't there more to your story, Kellen?" he asked. "It was not just that your mother wanted a boy, it was that she believed she'd had one."

That tale had been all over Thrush Hollow, so I was not

surprised he knew it. "Yes. She was traveling near Tambleham when her labor pains came on, and she had the baby at a roadside inn. Fortunately there was a midwife there who helped her through my birth. My mother always swore she stayed conscious long enough to see her baby, and he was a boy. Then she fainted, and was feverish for days. And by the time she was well and my father had brought her home, I was a boy no longer. She kept watching me, waiting for me to change back." I smiled. "But I never did."

Leona was staring at me. "Tambleham . . ." she said, her voice a whisper. "My brother was born in Tambleham."

"Is that right?" I said, since she seemed to think this was somehow significant. At least we had gotten off the topic of me and my charade. "You said your family moved around all the time, though, didn't you?"

Leona had her hand to her throat as if to force in breath or push back a scream. "Yes, we—every few years, we—but my aunt lived in Tambleham, and my mother wanted to be near her while she was pregnant with Phillip. My aunt was a midwife, you see."

I nodded. "Good to have family around at a time like that."

Leona shifted in her seat, showing some agitation. Even in the low light, I could see that her face had grown very pale. "I was ten when he was born," she continued. "I remember my mother screaming and crying."

"I've been present at a birthing or two," I said. "There's always some screaming."

Leona shook her head. "No, you don't understand. She

was crying *after* the baby was born. She was sobbing and sobbing, and nothing my aunt said would calm her down. I was in the other room with my hands over my ears, but I heard her say, 'I don't want her! Don't give her to me!' I know she said that. I know she said *her*."

For a long moment, neither Ayler nor I moved or spoke. "What happened then?" I asked in a very small voice.

"My aunt came out and told me to go over to the neighbor's. She said I should spend the night, and maybe even the next day or two. My father was gone for a few days, and there was no one to take care of me. She said she would come for me when my mother was feeling better."

"And?"

Leona shrugged. "So I did. Two days later, my aunt brought me home. My mother was lying in bed, nursing the baby. She looked so happy. She said, 'Leona, come in and meet your brother Phillip.' And I thought that was strange. Because I remembered what she had said before: 'I don't want *her*.' But then I thought I must have heard her wrong, or that my mother had misunderstood when my aunt first tried to give her the baby. I thought the baby must have been a boy all along."

"But maybe he wasn't," I said, and I could not bring my voice above a whisper.

"Maybe he wasn't," she echoed in a voice as quiet as mine. "When is your birthday, Kellen? Right before autumn, if I remember right."

"Exactly two months after Summermoon. I turned sixteen this year."

She was silent a moment. "Phillip's birthday. Phillip's age."

I said the words with a sense of wonder, still not believing they could be true. "Maybe *I* was the baby born to your mother late that summer. Maybe my own mother was right all along. Maybe she did give birth to a baby boy. If your aunt was midwife to both women, and my father was gone and so was yours, what would have prevented her from switching the children? Who would know any different? Who could offer proof?"

Now both of Leona's hands were on her cheeks. "Then—Kellen—but—does this mean you are my sister? That Phillip is not my brother after all? That you are—that you—but this is marvelous if it is true! Terrible and wonderful at the same time!"

My heart was so full that for a moment I could not speak. I could not help thinking of all the sad, wasted years of my mother's life, yearning for a child that she knew she had misplaced. Of the casual cruelty of two women who had conspired to swap infants, not caring what tragedies and tangles they set in motion. Of my own life, colored by attempts to be something I was not, bounded by my mother's disappointment and unease.

All of that swept away by my profound joy at suddenly, so unexpectedly, coming face-to-face with a sister who could love me no matter what shape I took.

"We will have to find a Truth-Teller," I said, my voice shaky. "Perhaps that disagreeable Eleda will come back in. She can let us know if we are in fact sisters, or if we have made up this wild story out of our own imaginations."

"No, it is entirely true," Ayler said in his soft voice. "Your aunt told me the tale fifteen years ago when I passed through Tambleham on my travels."

Now we both stared at him and he gave us back his abstracted smile. "You *knew*?" Leona demanded. "All this time, you *knew*? And you never told me, you never told Kellen—"

"It was a secret," he said apologetically. "The words would not cross my lips."

"Then how is it you can tell us the story now?" I said, pouncing a little.

He spread his hands; his smile widened. "I didn't tell you a thing," he replied. "You guessed it for yourselves."

"But you brought me here," I insisted. "You introduced me to Leona, knowing she was my sister. You must have thought—you must have hoped—"

"I am glad the story unfolded as it did," he admitted. "And perhaps I helped along its unraveling. But I told no secrets. I betrayed no confidences. How could I? I am a Safe-Keeper."

"I can't believe I have a sister," I said. "You have no idea how long I have wished and wished and *wished* for someone in my family to love me for who I am."

"And I for a sibling I could love!" Leona replied. Then she stopped short. "But that means—Phillip! What shall I tell him? He doesn't care much for me, but I'm all he has."

"He has my mother," I said. "Living in Thrush Hollow all these years, waiting for him to appear. Seeing him will be *her* dream come true."

"Still, it will be strange for him," Leona said. "To suddenly find out he has a different name, a different life—"

I laughed out loud. "Something tells me Phillip will be happy enough to trade his life for mine," I said. "He has just inherited five hundred gold pieces, after all."

Leona's eyes widened. "That's right! Your father's legacy! But will you really give up the money to Phillip?"

I shrugged. "The man I called my father left the money to his 'only living child.' Any Truth-Teller could tell you that's Phillip, not me. I suppose we could call Raymond in and have him argue the case for me, and probably win me at least half the money, but—Phillip has lost so much lately. I think I would like to see him win something. I even wished it for him earlier this afternoon."

"So many wishes come true all at once!" Leona said, exhaling a long sigh of breath. "And we haven't even burned the wreath yet!"

"Wintermoon magic operates by its own logic," Ayler said. "But I would say you had both cherished some powerful dreams."

Leona smiled at me. "Time to think up some new ones, then," she said.

"Not quite yet," I said, smiling back at my sister. "I'm still getting used to these."

Chase and Ayler started the bonfire while Gryffin sat there with the wreath across his lap. Sallie snuck over from her parents' house just before we threw the greenery into the fire—because, as she said, she wanted to see her particular wishes turn to smoke across the moon. She goggled when she saw me, wearing one of Leona's dresses and boldly holding Gryffin's hand, and then she laughed and cried when we told her the story.

"There will never be another Wintermoon like this one!" she exclaimed, throwing her arms first around me, then around Leona. By this time, she had gotten into the spirit of it, so she hugged Chase and Gryffin and Ayler while she was at it. I thought I saw Ayler hold the embrace a little longer than she had expected, and I thought I saw her smile up at him with an expression of happy surprise.

"I have had plenty of bountiful Wintermoons before this one," I murmured in Gryffin's ear. "I am not ready to say this is my finest Wintermoon ever."

He laughed and kissed me lightly on the mouth. "Then that will be my wish," he replied. "That every Wintermoon be better than the last."

Not a realistic wish, as anyone could have told him—but I would not be the one to say so. Why limit your dreams, after all? Why not hope for the grandest and the best? I watched Chase throw the wreath into the bonfire, and I saw the flames scrawl secrets on the sky, and I closed my eyes and knew no end of dreaming.

Turn the page for a sneak peek at
Sharon Shinn's brand-new romance—

GENERAL WINSTON'S
Daughter

When seventeen-year-old heiress Averie Winston
travels with her guardian to farway Chiarrin, she
looks forward to the reunion with her father, who is a
commanding general; seeing her handsome fiance,
Morgan; and exploring the strange new country. What
she finds is entirely different from what she expected.
Although the Chiarizzi appear to accept the invading
army, rebels have already tried to destroy them;
Morgan is not the man she thought he was; and she
finds herself falling in love with Lieutenant Ket
Du'kai, who himself comes from a conquered society.
Can the irrepressible Averie remake herself in this
new world?

CHAPTER
ONE

It seemed like the voyage to Chiarrin would take forever. Three weeks out of Port Elise, Averie could hardly remember a time she had not lived aboard ship, sharing cramped quarters with Lady Selkirk, eating progressively less interesting meals in the captain's private dining room, and spending hours at the stern watching the water unfold. Her books and sewing projects could entertain her for only a few hours a day, and she and Lady Selkirk could exhaust their common topics of conversation before breakfast.

If she had not had Lieutenant Du'kai's companionship, she truly thought she might have gone mad.

At first, Lady Selkirk had not been sure Lieutenant Du'kai was suitable company for a gently bred young girl. Averie had watched with some amusement as her chaperone visibly weighed up his advantages and drawbacks. Against him was the fact that he was Xantish, with that characteristic brown skin and curly dark hair, and completely without ties to any of the prominent families in Xan'tai. In his favor was the fact that he was an officer in the Aeberelle army with a promising future before him.

What ultimately made Lady Selkirk welcome him into their circle, Averie thought, was the sheer unrelenting boredom of the journey. There were so few people to talk to aboard the frigate, and certainly no one who could offer entertaining conversation. Lieutenant Du'kai had been a godsend. By the second week out, neither Averie nor Lady Selkirk would think to sit down to dinner without inviting him to join them.

"You only want to take your meals with us because our food is so much better than what they serve the enlisted men," Averie said playfully one night.

The accusation made him smile. He had a particularly attractive smile, which lit his whole face and made his warm brown eyes seem even warmer. "I would gladly accept a dinner invitation from you if you were serving fried cat and desert grass," he said gallantly. His Aebrian was as fluent as hers, though he spoke with a faint accent, exotic and appealing. "It is the company, not the food, that draws me back."

Averie giggled, but Lady Selkirk nodded. "Very properly said," she approved. She was dressed tonight in a gown of dark purple; she seemed, by her bulk, to be anchoring the table to the floor. Her iron-gray hair was pulled back into a no-nonsense bun, but she had allowed herself the frivolity of earrings and a single gold necklace.

Lieutenant Du'kai, of course, was very neat in his dark blue uniform with its silver buttons. But Averie had not bothered to take much trouble with her appearance. She was wearing a thin pink cotton dress, and even that seemed heavy for the weather, which grew hotter and more humid the farther south they traveled. She had dispensed with the underdress she would have been expected to wear in Port Elise. Her blonde hair hung in a careless braid over her left shoulder, long enough to brush the table. If she'd thought Lady Selkirk would have allowed it, she'd have come barefoot to the meal.

"Well, I wouldn't eat fried cat with anyone, even if I liked him," Averie said.

Lieutenant Du'kai smiled at her again. "Ah, if you plan to travel the world, you will have to accustom yourself to eating much worse meals."

Averie spooned mashed apples onto her plate. "Such as?" she demanded.

"Some cultures consider insects a delicacy," he said.

"To eat?" she exclaimed. "I don't believe you."

"I assure you, it is true. Ants and locusts and crickets."

Lady Selkirk looked horrified, but Averie was intrigued. "How do they taste?"

"It depends on what sauces and seasonings you use to prepare them. Crickets, I know, can be covered in chocolate and eaten as a dessert. Very crunchy."

"You've tried them?"

"I was in Khovstu for a year. I ate them often. Quite tasty."

"I don't want to eat crickets no matter what they're covered with," Averie said.

Lady Selkirk sniffed. She was a champion sniffer. It was the way she signaled that she considered a topic, or an outfit, or a situation, so far from genteel that it should not even be acknowledged. "This apple compote is very good," she said pointedly.

"It is," Lieutenant Du'kai agreed.

But Averie was not willing to see the subject turned. "Do you eat insects in Xan'tai?" she wanted to know.

"No, indeed, we eat many of the same foods you enjoy in Aeberelle," he replied. "There are variations, of course. We do not grow much wheat, so we make our bread with a different grain. And we grow spices that are unfamiliar to you northern folk."

"Not anymore!" Averie said. "Everyone has been using ma'het in their meat dishes lately. I like it very much."

"Much more subtle than salt," Lady Selkirk said.

Lieutenant Du'kai was smiling again. "Yes, and the Aebrians' taste for ma'het is proving to be quite a boon to the farmers in the eastern provinces of Xan'tai," he said. "It has made a handful of old families very rich."

"What else is different?" Averie wanted to know. "In Xan'tai?" They had talked very little about his home country in all these days, she suddenly realized. She had not even thought to question him about the country where he had been born.

"Oh, that is a conversation that could take days!" he said in a teasing voice.

Averie thought, *He does not want to talk about it. Or at least he does not want to talk about it with us.* Which piqued her interest even more. "No, truly, tell us something," she urged. "I know that it is much warmer there, and that you have many rivers and flatlands. But I don't know anything about the people or what they do."

He considered her briefly, and for a moment she saw something in his dark eyes that startled her—sadness, perhaps, or weariness, or resignation. It surprised her even more than his reluctance to talk. What did Lieutenant Du'kai have to be unhappy about? "Or what they eat or what they wear," he added. "There is too much to tell."

"One thing," she wheedled.

He glanced around the room, as if looking for something that would spark an idea, and his gaze rested briefly on her left hand, lifted to hold a teacup. "Your ring," he said.

She set down the cup and wiggled her hand, so the large ruby on her fourth finger sparkled in the candle-light. "It's very pretty, isn't it?" she said. "It belonged to Morgan's mother."

Lieutenant Du'kai nodded and said, "And it indicates that you and Colonel Stode are betrothed."

Averie dimpled. She still liked to hear the words said aloud. "Yes, but we have been engaged forever. I think I was eight when I decided I would marry him. He was seventeen and thought I was just a horrid little girl, but I always knew. I was probably fifteen before he began to fall in love with me, but it was a year before he proposed."

"That's hardly forever," Lieutenant Du'kai said. "You're only seventeen now."

"Eighteen!" she exclaimed. "I had my birthday right before we set sail. But what were you going to say about my ring?"

"In Xan'tai, couples do not exchange jewelry to signify that they are married or about to be," said Lieutenant Du'kai. "Nor is it as easy to tell by dress what a man's station in life is."

That made Lady Selkirk sniff again. She was a great believer in being able to determine a person's worth by his clothing and appearance. But Averie was curious.

"It's not? Then how do you find out about people?"

"They tell you!" he said with a laugh. "The first time you are introduced to someone, he will give you his whole history in a few sentences. 'I am Ket Du'kai. I am twenty-five years old. I have no wife; my parents are both still living. I have no independent fortune, but I am honorably employed as a soldier in the Aeberelle army.' And you nod, and then you give him your own history in return."

"I am Averie Winston, *eighteen* years old. My mother is dead, but my father is alive and he is the top general in the Aeberelle army," she rattled off, although Lady Selkirk turned a scandalized look upon her. One simply did not *discuss* one's attributes; one just assumed everyone knew them. "I have quite an impressive fortune, actually—"

"Averie!" Lady Selkirk hissed.

Averie continued blithely. "Although it won't be mine until I'm twenty-one. Or until my father dies, and then I'd be quite rich, but of course I'd be very sad."

"Averie Agatha Winston!" Lady Selkirk exclaimed. She was aghast.

"It's not like Lieutenant Du'kai doesn't know I'm an heiress," Averie said.

"It is cheap and vulgar to say so aloud," Lady Selkirk said in a crushing voice.

"But not to Lieutenant Du'kai," Averie reminded her.

"I was just pretending I was meeting him for the first time in Xan'tai."

Lady Selkirk turned her hard gray eyes toward the corporal. "Forgive her lapse in manners," she said. "She is something of a hoyden, despite my best efforts."

"I am not at all offended," he assured her. He spoke gravely, but Averie thought he was hiding a smile. "In fact, she has not finished telling me her status."

"What? What else should I have said?"

"You should have mentioned that you are engaged. A young man in Xan'tai who meets you for the first time will want to know if you are eligible for courting."

Averie smiled. "I am engaged to be married to Colonel Morgan Stode—now, do I tell you *his* status, too?"

"You don't have to, but it would generally be of interest to your listeners."

"He doesn't have a fortune, but he's been in the army for nearly ten years, and he's risen quite rapidly through the ranks," she said.

"His family is of the highest respectability, but there was a tragedy involving his father," Lady Selkirk broke in to explain. Obviously she couldn't stand the thought of anyone thinking Averie would marry a penniless man of no particular breeding.

"Shot himself and left behind nothing but debts," Averie explained.

"*Averie!*"

"Well, Lieutenant Du'kai doesn't care," Averie said. "I don't either. And it's not like it was Morgan's fault. He was only ten or eleven when his father died. His sisters went to be governesses," she added, "but as soon as he had enough income, he bought them a little house in the country and they didn't have to work anymore. I like them both a great deal, but they're always criticizing my behavior."

"Perhaps if you behaved better, they would have no incentive to do so," Lady Selkirk shot out. She turned her mortified face toward their guest. "You must be quite shocked this evening, Lieutenant, at Averie's irrepressible mood. I assure you, she is not always so wild."

"I'm not *wild*! I haven't done anything wrong! What have I done?"

Lieutenant Du'kai gave Lady Selkirk a little bow. He was seated across from her at the small table, still cluttered with all their plates and dishes. "Indeed, I would never find her high spirits out of place. In fact, I was about to be bold enough to ask you about your own history, for I do not know how you became Lady Averie's chaperone. I would not expect you to give me a Xantish introduction, of course! Just some details."

His gentle tone mollified her, as it always did, and Lady Selkirk responded with a smile that was almost pleased. "Oh, my own story is very ordinary. I married a fine man and had two sons. I have known the Winstons forever—my father's property runs alongside their principal estate—and General Winston's dear wife died when Averie was only ten. There was no one else to take care of this child."

"There were plenty of people," Averie said with a scowl. In fact, she hadn't noticed much of a difference in her life once her mother died, except that she had even more freedom. Her mother had been vain, beautiful, and mostly absent. Averie had been left to roam the estates pretty much on her own, which had suited her just fine.

"My husband had died a few years before," Lady Selkirk went on. "So when General Winston asked me if I would help raise Averie, I happily agreed. At first, I was installed at Weymire Estate, but lately we have spent more time in Port Elise, where I have tried to prepare Averie for the life she will lead when she is wed." She sighed. "It has not been an easy task."

Averie took her turn to sniff. "It could have been easier," she informed her chaperone. "*I* didn't care about deportment or learning how to speak Weskish! When am I ever going to go to Weskolia, anyway, since we've been at war with them forever! And Morgan wouldn't care, either, if I was not so *accomplished* in all those silly social arts."

Lady Selkirk turned that cool gaze on her. "Indeed, Colonel Stode would care a great deal," she said in a steely voice. "He is an ambitious man, and he could have a spectacular political career ahead of him once he leaves the army. He will need a wife of much charm and social skill to aid him in that career."

Averie glared down at her plate, suddenly in a bad mood, for Lady Selkirk was right. Morgan was ambitious. He *did* hope to have a career in government. Averie eventually would have to learn how to be a political wife.

"I cannot see that either of you has a thing to worry about," Lieutenant Du'kai said in a soothing voice. "From what I can tell, Lady Averie is both well mannered and absolutely genuine, and I would think she would win friends for Colonel Stode no matter what company they find themselves in."

Such a remark could not help but please both members of his audience, and Averie and Lady Selkirk both found themselves beaming. At that very moment, the cook's assistant squeezed into the dining room, bearing a tray of lemon tarts. Sugar was bound to improve anyone's mood, and they ended the meal quite in charity with one another. Averie was already looking forward to tomorrow night's dinner.